The Roots That Clutch

# THE ROOTS THAT CLUTCH

Beth Ann Hooper

**TOWER** *of* **BABEL**

ISBN paperback edition: 979-8-9912927-0-2
ISBN ebook: 979-8-9912927-1-9

Cover photo: Askin Tulay Over, iStockphoto
Graphic design: Puntspatie [bno], Amsterdam, The Netherlands


Also by the same author:
*Lot* (Dutch version of *The Roots That Clutch*)

www.therootsthatclutch.com

This novel is based on my own true story about how I found out a family secret that was crucial to my identity, my father's and my children's. Even as a young child, I had the sense that something wasn't right and when any of us children asked questions about our heritage, we would get vague answers or overly dramatic reactions that would shock us into silence. And there was a definite difference between my mother's side of the family and my father's. At least, my mother's side of the family would tell us something about the pieces of the puzzle we had to put together, while my father's side left us with nothing but the air we breathed.

But the apple never falls far from the tree even if it is hidden. Never did I imagine that my academic research would provide the answers for a child's probing curiosity. That I would learn my family history from strangers on the other side of the world. Life likes to throw you left curve balls when you least expect it.

Because of my discoveries, I now live in a part of the world where I have 400 years of family history on my father's side of the family available to me. My neighbors and distant cousins tell me my family history with more subdued emotion and sometimes even enthusiasm. Having roots somewhere is a good thing. Clutch them tightly.

*Beth Ann Hooper*

*What are the roots that clutch, what branches grow*

From *The Waste Land*




*Earth's axle creaks; the year jolts on; the trees*
*begin to slip their brittle leaves, their flakes of rust;*
*and darkness takes the edge off daylight, not*
*because it wants to – never that. Because it must.*

*And you? Your life was not your own to keep...*

From "Mythology", Andrew Motion

A Turkish girl cleans hotel rooms for her summer job. In one of the rooms, she finds a manuscript left behind by an American tourist. A student of English literature, in the fall she brings it to one of her professors at the University of Ankara.

They are shocked by the contents.


> Oh Mr. Eliot
> Fear the hooded hordes swarming over endless plains
> Oh Mr. Eliot
> Fear the present decay of eastern Europe
>
> Oh Mr. Eliot
> Fear the Amazons

"You've got to do something with that!" the elderly Jewish professor exclaimed as he stood opposite Jane and shook his finger at her purse. Both of them stood outside Penn University Club at the corner of an intersection in downtown Philadelphia after what had obviously been a very fruitful lunch. It seemed rather unreal that a previously un-revealed personal connection in modern literary history could be so easily wrapped up and tucked away like a personal item in a woman's purse.

But there it was

Unreal

Unreal

Dr. Rochdale, bearded, bespectacled, British and lover of brown suits, always had his students write a short essay on one of a list of works he had randomly selected as their first literature assignment at university. Jane chose W.H. Auden's poem, "Autumn Song" from what Dr. Rochdale had selected.

Jane approached the poem like she did all poems because she had the audacity, some might call it the American audacity, to think that she could read it herself. She let the meaning of the words come to her intuitively. If she couldn't grasp the meaning or diction of a word, she looked it up until she found a definition that fit within the context of the rest of the poem.

She had no idea that Auden was a homosexual although Dr. Rochdale didn't believe that. But apparently her reading of the poem wasn't what everyone else thought.

"Miss Hooper, could you remain after class please?" Dr. Rochdale asked with that Oxfordian curtness. While everyone left, he handed the essay to her.

"I wanted to give you back your essay so you could look at it, but I was wondering, could I keep it for another week?"

"Yes, of course."

"Well, good. Go ahead, read my comments quickly." Dr. Rochdale had one of those voices that did not need a megaphone, but he knew how to adjust the volume enough so that you would not be able to accuse him of not needing one.

"Auden's homosexuality is, of course, no secret. However, your reading of this poem is extraordinary. You could be right."

He allowed her a moment to let his comments sink in. Though the moment of silence amounted to not much more than a split second, she was grateful for it.

"Now you and I both know Auden was a homosexual."

"I didn't. Really I didn't. I figured it out through the poem."

"How did you get to this reading then?"

"I had the feeling the word 'trolls' was the key to the rest of the poem. I looked it up in six dictionaries. The Collins said one connotation of 'trolling' was homosexual slang for wandering through the park to pick up a sexual partner."

He turned his head and seemingly looked down at his notes in silence.

He turned and looked at her again. "Why are you here?" Then, turning his face away from her and with a flustered and irritated tone, "Oh, you probably have a boyfriend here or something."

"No, I'm here because I want to be here." She had rushed her answer to satisfy him.

Again he looked down at his notes in silence. And then he feigned asking for announcing, "I would like to keep your essay until next week. Alright?" It was one of those alrights that assumed she had already concurred.

"Sure, no problem."

"Alright, then. Goodbye."

"Goodbye."

She left the room quietly and harbored a feeling that she had done something wrong, but she had no idea what. Dr. Rochdale stared down at his notes again, not turning his head as university tutors and college professors always do as a way of asserting their authority and to let you know that acknowledgement of you depends on them.

It was not until Jane was older that she realized that every relationship requires two parties and that a teacher cannot teach anything unless there are students present. A teacher learns, and especially a university scholar, that he will only be able to look at his subject in a cubbyholed way unless he is confronted with that fresh, new and uninhibited approach that his students' inexperience brings to him. As if they must remind him that new life is still within his grasps and is still his for the taking.

Jane's dad stood across from her and looked down at the books and notebooks scattered around the lounge chair she occupied along the side of the swimming pool. He hadn't said anything yet about her quitting political science the year before and starting English this year.

"You're getting some good reading done there."

She looked up and saw the Arizona mountains against the late afternoon sky behind him. "Thanks." She should have smiled when he said that, but she always felt uneasy about being too enthusiastic about anything in front of her dad.

He must be happy to have a visitor during the holiday season after he came home from work, she thought. His girlfriend didn't like to go to his apartment, so he would always end up going to her house. Even now in the new life he had chosen for himself, his perpetual sense of emptiness would be the only thing that would follow him.

Jane and her dad had grabbed a last minute flight to spend Christmas with her grandmother. One morning, Jane was going on some intellectual tangent and kept ruminating about some historical or literary fact of some kind when she walked into her grandmother's tiny living room from the guest room she had slept in the night before. Her grandmother sat erect in the middle of her loveseat and smiled silently and surreptitiously, surrounded by her quaint, porcelain ladies' statuettes and historical prints of Nantucket hanging on the wall behind her. A room so full of memorabilia and family history, but which completely lacked any family pictures. Jane's grandmother stared at Jane with such a peaceful gaze of reminiscence; one that wanders back into time to resurrect the synesthesia of a timeless experience that only those who partook of that experience can remember and enjoy.

Jane had never seen her gaze like that before. Her dad's family always seemed like jittery amateur actors in a play that was way over their heads. Just one moment of silence would evoke such a nervous sense of indiscretion; it had to be avoided at all costs.

Dr. Rochdale had summoned Jane to his office. She wasn't following any of his courses so she had no idea what it was about.

"Beatrice Smith asked me to speak to you. We are very concerned you may quit your studies here."

Jane was really taken aback. She was not the type of student anyone took under their wing.

"How do you know Beatrice?" Dr. Rochdale asked.

"I babysit for her."

"You know she used to be a student here, too?"

"Yes, I do." Miss Smith was now a tutor at the English department and like Dr. Rochdale herself from England. Though her dream was to teach literature, she had been teaching English language acquisition and English presentation skills at the Faculty of Medicine for years. Like a migrant worker who could only find a menial job to support his family despite the skills he brought from home, Miss Smith had the tedious task of teaching medical students how to present their work to their future peers while she completed her dissertation on T.S. Eliot and raised her family with her Dutch husband who was never home. No such courses existed at the English department or any of the Faculty of Arts departments for that matter, as if it was assumed and prescribed that none of the students would be doing research any time soon.

"And you saw her at the Christmas party?"

"Yes."

"What did you tell her?"

"I just said I don't feel like anyone is interested in my ideas here. I thought university was going to be different. I feel like all I do is regurgitate what I learn in class for exams. I wanted to learn how to write poetry."

"So, you write poetry."

"Sometimes."

"Have you ever been published?"

"No."

"Can't you go back to the States?"

"No, not right now."

"Why not? Don't you have any family there?"

"Yes, I do, but it's not a good time to go back right now." Luckily, Dr. Rochdale didn't question her any further. For once, his Oxbridge sense of discretion came in handy. She didn't want to tell him that her parents had been going through an acrimonious divorce for a long time, something that had been waiting to happen for years but didn't happen until she and two other sisters were about to go to college. Any money saved for continuing their education consequently ended up financing their parents' attorneys' fees. A few years before Jane had started university in the Netherlands, she had been a high school exchange student there, and quickly realized if she could get into the country's social system, she didn't have to be financially dependent on her parents anymore. An artist's son helped her get her residency papers in the Netherlands where they only had to prove they lived together and didn't have to marry so she could stay. The immigration law had been created to give foreign homosexuals the same rights as foreign heterosexuals, because at that time, homosexuals could not marry, and therefore had no other way of living with their Dutch partner. It also inadvertently saved her from the same fate as her parents' once she had her papers.

"Have you considered applying for a Harting scholarship and going to the UK for a year?"

"I have, yes."

"Good. Make an appointment with me in early March so that we can discuss your shortlist of universities. I can't guarantee which university you'll get but we'll see what we can do."

Jane was looking for a reason to stay in the UK. The tutors talked to you here. The students and professors actually discussed topics here. It was a far cry from the authoritarian attitude she had grown accustomed to in Leiden where the tutors just told you what you needed to know for your exam because they assumed you weren't going to ask any questions anyway. Their authoritarian attitude also maintained their pecking order. In Leiden, the tutors never ran the risk that their students would outshine them.

It was an utterly uninspiring environment to be educated in. Ideas weren't important and definitely not new ones. Dr. Rochdale had done her a real service by suggesting Manchester as a university to attend for her Harting scholarship. So that's how she ended up in Manchester, eternally grateful to Dr. Rochdale for finding a way to inspire her to continue to studying literature.

It's funny how these smug English accents always end up having so much influence on lives that had declared themselves independent so long ago, she mused one morning while sitting outside the University of Manchester library. In the beginning we are all so overly impressed with their eloquence. Apparently, they have larger vocabularies than we do. But once the novelty wears off, and you realize their eloquence hides the socio-cultural straitjacket they must survive in, you are relieved you are not one of them.

We Yanks don't understand there are things that are just not done, she thought. We go ahead and do it anyway. They call it cowboy or maverick. It's an attitude that has worked pretty well for us, but one that totally threatens the English sense of order. Other Europeans' sense of order for that matter, too. Against the grain. And they can't stand it, she thought to herself.

So she decided to try and stay in Manchester because at least they talked to you here, unlike the Dutch where four hundred years after his death, William the Silent remained the national hero. Jane asked her Victorian poetry tutor whether she should try and stay to do a master's or MPHIL that she could expand into a PhD.

"Yes! Why not? Do you need a supervisor?"

"Yeah, I guess I do. But I don't know what I should do for a topic."

"Oh I know what you can do. Eliot and the 1890s poets."

"Oh, ok. But shouldn't I include Pound? Can you really leave him out of it?"

"If that's what you think then you've got to include him."

"I've always wondered why Eliot gets all the attention."

"Look into it. I'd be happy to be your supervisor. It will give me an excuse to drop a part-time student I've had for years. I must have read a million words of his because he keeps rewriting his work. It's a real never-ending story, I'm afraid."

She felt a pang of sorrow for the part-time student. He was just trying to get it right.

She decided not to stay in Manchester after an Australian tutor in Leiden warned her about the way things worked in the UK.

"After years of work a committee decides right then and there whether you pass or fail. Here the committee makes recommendations for revisions, and you revise and then turn it in again to defend. But the outcome has been decided by then. I was on a committee once in the UK where one professor walked in and was hell-bent on failing the candidate. That's exactly what he did. The candidate had put years of effort into this. I was utterly appalled."

Her Australian tutor's warning about the viciousness of academic politics led her to choose the more secure location for the time being. Jane kept the topic and used it for her master's thesis in Leiden.

Jane must have called Dr. Rochdale twenty times that morning before he answered.

"Did you call me several times this morning?" he asked.

"No. I didn't."

"Well, why are you calling?"

"I was wondering whether you'd agree to be the first reader on my master's."

"Haven't you asked Professor Stanford? He's an American like you."

"He's on sabbatical and he recommended you for the subject matter," she explained.

"What's your topic?"

"Eliot, Pound and their late-nineteenth century British predecessors."

"Oh, good topic." He caught himself and let a well-timed pause break up his sudden enthusiasm. Dr. Rochdale returned to his usual curtness. "Which 1890s poets are you looking at?"

"Umm. Symons, Davidson and Thomson. Maybe Johnson and Dowson, too."

"Make sure you look at Henley. Who's your second reader?"

"I don't have one yet."

"Ask Dr. Lebenstein. He's writing a book on Pound. Put your proposal in my pigeonhole after you've spoken to him. Goodbye."

"Thank you. Bye."

That Oxbridge curtness always knew how to erase your composure. His simplest question could make you stumble.

That night Jane called Dr. Lebenstein, totally unprepared for his German brusqueness.

"I thought you didn't like me."

JEEZ. How do you get out of that one? "But you're a good tutor," she answered quickly to try and save the conversation.

Dr. Lebenstein, German originally and a classicist, and Jane had a history. He had asked her once after class whether she had abolished lipstick that week. Dumbstruck and infuriated by his question, the only answer she could give him was a cold, dark stare of shock and indignation, which he answered with the flustered wave of an apologetic hand. Immature as she was, she couldn't forgive him that semester. She challenged him during every tutorial that semester and undercut any argument he presented with a better one. During a departmental dinner after a poetry reading which students could also attend, he claimed he was a Jungian. Jane sat directly opposite him and told him she sincerely doubted that and thought he was a Freudian based on his tutorials. Spooked by her accusation, he left the dinner early.

"Who's your first reader?"

"Dr. Rochdale. He and Professor Stanford recommended you because you're writing a book on Pound."

"Hm." Pause. "Alright, when you submit your proposal to Dr. Rochdale, put a copy in my pigeonhole."

That autumn Jane took a few courses just to get out of the house in between researching her master's. She didn't need the credits thanks to Dr. Rochdale's good advice that she should go abroad for awhile. She had accumulated enough credits in Manchester so that when she came back, she only had to write her thesis.

She took a course in modern American literature. Just before class and while the students waited for the tutor to arrive, Jane read the introduction about the other American Modernist poet William Carlos Williams in the anthology they used. It said he was a lifelong resident of Rutherford, New Jersey, and he had been a doctor there for forty years in addition to being a great poet.

Rutherford? How many times had she not heard the name of that town during her childhood? Her dad grew up there. Her grandmother had been a passionate English teacher. Her dad was a sportswriter before he was a lobbyist, but he always kept writing and broadcasting. They must have run into this poet. Funny they had never mentioned him. She had even been baptized in Rutherford though they lived all the way in Florida at that time. That was a big trip for a young family in 1969, even if they did fly.

She didn't finish the course after that class. She felt she should concentrate on the poets who never returned to America voluntarily.

"So what's your master's on?" Jane's mom was planning to come over from the States for her graduation.

"Poets." That's all she would tell her. Your master's thesis didn't seem like something you should discuss with your mother.

"Oh, your father was delivered by a poet." Jane nearly dropped the phone but didn't let the receiver fall, because even though she sensed what her mother was going to say next, she didn't want to leave anything to chance.

"Williams or something," said her mother lightly.

Jane stood on the San Francisco hilltop and gazed at the Golden Gate Bridge. She had always wanted to travel through the great national parks out west and come to San Francisco and see Haight Ashbury to celebrate finishing her master's and that's exactly what she did.

Her boyfriend, who was soon to become her future husband, did not want to go with her, so she went on her own. It was the first omen, but at that time she was not listening. Instead, she was writing poetry.

**HAIGHT ASHBURY**
Jerry Garcia died sometime around the time
I was in San Francisco.
Kurt Cobain had died some time before.

Both deaths untimely.

Yet, Garcia, fattened with hedonism
His organs weakened from years of drug abuse,
Died of a heart attack.
The baby boomers mourned his death and lamented
the loss and hailed him as one of the greats.

Great what? Parasite?

Kurt Cobain, our whole generation did not even have the time
    to become
Parasitic, only just enough time to self-implode
Dreams promised that never materialized,
shattered in the hands of hedonistic predecessors, our futures
    snuffed out our grasps, at the expense of our parents' carnal
    desires and need for sedation.

And at Haight Ashbury
The runaways sit in a row along the street in front
    of McDonald's,
My generation's death row,
All seeking the solace of exile,
And instead finding the exclusion of pariahs and a more
    pervasive solitude.

And I, knowing how close
I came to being one of them,
Saw, sitting on the ground,
Such much like Kurt Cobain
Long, blond hair
blue eyes
pleading
"Could you spare some change?"
He, seeing he had caught my eye
I did not respond but walked on feigning I had never seen him
    but he was much quicker than I was
"Could you spare me a smile?"

And with that request, he ripped my heart from between
    my breasts.

Jane decided to start her PhD five years after her master's. During those preceding years, she had worked as a writer in the oil industry where they taught her how to write clearly, simply and succinctly, and she had learned the real practicalities of writing. But doing that PhD was always in the back of her mind even after she had married and been transferred to Houston, Texas. She decided to go back to the Netherlands with her Dutch husband and give it a shot.

She asked Professor Stanford to be her advisor. He agreed wholeheartedly, but said she needed a Modernism expert and nineteenth century expert for day-to-day guidance. He suggested Dr. Lebenstein again, as well as an Italian-born scholar, Dr. Ungaro. Dr. Rochdale was set to retire the following year and could no longer offer his guidance though he offered his help at any time. "I'm still around," he promised.

After the matter of readers was settled, Professor Stanford gave Jane some scholarly advice. "Find a way to make Modernism international."

Jane visited the Amsterdam University Library because she could just pull the books off of the shelf and borrow them. Leiden only allowed students to borrow books in the underground storage space. The books on the shelves were off-limits, especially to students.

She had already prepared herself for the fact that the complete works of the most important British poets in her research, W.E. Henley, Arthur Symons and James Thomson, were not available in the Netherlands and the closest place she could get them was the British Library in London. Luckily, Davidson's complete works were available from Amsterdam which led her to go there. She had used an anthology of 1890s poetry for her master's thesis from the Middelburg library in the province of Zeeland. That just wasn't going to cut it for a PhD.

She walked through the shelves bemoaning the newest daunting mess she had gotten herself into, when W.E. Henley's complete works caught her eye, all eight volumes of them. But there were red and yellow dot stickers on the bottom of the books' backs. She rushed to the "s" to see whether she could find Symons. All nine volumes of his complete works were there and a biography with yellow dot stickers on the bottom of the backs. She went to the "t". No Thomson. She grabbed a copy of one of Symons' volumes and one of Henley's and stumbled to the front desk.

"May I ask a question?"

A middle-aged Dutch woman, complete with gray hair cut in a bob, stared down at Jane over her reading glasses. Jane had obviously intruded upon the librarian's tasks.

"Yes?"

"What do the red and yellow dots mean?"

"The yellow dots mean the books will be stored away in an archive and difficult to borrow. The red dots mean the books are going to be destroyed."

"What? You can't destroy them! I need them for my dissertation. The closest copies are in London."

Relieved that the purpose of her life's work had finally presented itself, the librarian burst out this advice, "Then you've got to check them out and just keep on borrowing them forever! I know you should never destroy books, especially in an arts faculty, and I've told them over and over again! But it's a new university policy. They want to build a campus and save on space so they're destroying books they don't think are important. But they can't! They shouldn't! I know they shouldn't! What if someone needs them for their dissertation, like you?

"Look here," she pointed to a bookcase next to the front desk. "The public library burned down in Lyon. Everything was lost. I'm saving the books the university wants to destroy and I'm sending them to Lyon! How can they do this? It takes years of effort to build a collection, and after years of guarding and maintaining this collection, they are throwing out my books like wrapping paper! Just check out the books and keep checking them out forever, as long as you need them. Anything to keep them from being destroyed. If you have any problems ever, just contact me. How can they do this! What if someone needs these books for their dissertation?" Her student assistant looked up and smiled.

Jane went and got the twenty-one volumes she needed. When she got back to the front desk, the librarian gave Jane three of her own plastic bags so that Jane could protect the books from the rain that threatened from the overcast sky outside.

Jane wrote a lot that summer, really what she had done for her master's and got burned at her first appointment with her readers. The demands of a PhD are much greater than a master's and she had to go through the same rite of passage everyone else does. The first meeting with Dr. Lebenstein and Dr. Ungaro after she wrote her first chapter had the makings of a World War II interrogation.

Dr. Lebenstein: "Is this what you're turning in for a first chapter?"

Dr. Ungaro to Dr. Lebenstein: "I don't think she realizes what she's getting into."

Dr. Lebenstein: "You can't just throw away what everyone else has done."

Dr. Ungaro: "Yes, keep looking at Baudelaire, but you must also look at Dante."

Dr. Lebenstein: "Are you saying Dante and Baudelaire DIDN'T influence Eliot and Pound and actually only the 1890s poets did?"

Dr. Ungaro: "And you'll have to have some kind of theory involved for your framework. You can't just go without."

Dr Lebenstein: "Yes, take a look at Genette's intertextuality."

Dr. Ungaro: "Dr. Rochdale always advised you to look at W.E. Henley. Have you done that yet?"

Dr. Lebenstein: "So you're saying W.E. Henley, John Davidson, James Thomson and Arthur Symons were the most important influences from the 1890s on Eliot and Pound? What about the other 1890s poets? Are you going to leave them completely to the wayside?"

Dr. Ungaro: "How can you just leave out Yeats?"

Dr. Lebenstein: "I cannot believe she has not even mentioned Yeats!" Yeats was the subject of Dr. Lebenstein's dissertation. She had committed a mortal sin.

It is no use mentioning the answers she tried to get in. Every effort to reassure them was futile. She would just have to rewrite the chapter.

Dr. Lebenstein: "Read the poetry. Then reread the poetry. Then set it aside for awhile. Suddenly, it will hit you."

"Ok. I'll take to your advice to heart. May I ask a question before we finish? I think I may have found an appropriate title for my dissertation."

"Yes, go ahead. Tell us," Dr. Ungaro encouraged her. "What is it?"

"The Roots That Clutch."

"Ooh, good title, Jane!" exclaimed Dr. Ungaro.

"Yes, I agree!" Dr. Lebenstein concurred enthusiastically. "Straight from *The Waste Land*. Good thinking, Jane!"

Dr. Rochdale asked Jane to read at one of the department poetry evenings. The evening's theme was Oscar Wilde and his contemporaries. Jane decided to read Henley's "Operation" after she had given a short introduction on the poet and his work. She thought she would also make Dr. Rochdale happy because she had listened to his advice.

"William Ernest Henley was born on August 23, 1849, in Gloucester, England, son of a bookseller. At the age of twelve, he was diagnosed with what probably would have been tubercular arthritis. Victorian surgeons amputated the limbs of such patients, but amputation in those days usually meant certain death because of gangrene. In 1867, at the age of eighteen, Henley's foot was amputated and miraculously, he survived. Fortunately, Henley was spared another operation until 1873, when he was put under the care of Joseph Lister at the Royal Edinburgh Infirmary for twenty months. Henley's case was exactly what Lister was looking for so he could test his theories of antiseptic surgery. During his treatment of Henley, Lister scraped the infection from his patient's bones in a series of operations. It was his experiences in the Royal Edinburgh Infirmary that led Henley to write a collection of poems called *In Hospital*.

"Henley is best known as one of the most adamant Anti-Decadents of the 1890s and was opposed to Oscar Wilde's theories of art. As editor of the *National Observer*, he was the head of what Beerbohm called the Henley Regatta, which included such Anti-Decadent writers as Kipling. Henley's *National Observer* held nothing back when it denounced Wilde and the theory of art he stood for, and here is a quote from an article in the *National Observer* which was printed right after the arrest of Oscar Wilde:

'There is not a man or woman in the English-speaking world possessed of the treasure of a wholesome mind who is not under a deep debt of gratitude to the Marquess of Queensberry for destroying the High Priest of the Decadents. The obscene impostor, whose prominence has been a social outrage ever since he transferred from Trinity Dublin to Oxford his vices, his follies, and his vanities, has been exposed, and that thoroughly at last. But to the exposure there must be legal and social sequels. There must be another trial at the Old Bailey, or a coroner's inquest – the latter for choice; and of the Decadents, of their hideous conceptions of the meaning of Art, of their worse than Eleusinian mysteries, there must be an absolute end.'"

Jane decided to give the audience some comic relief and make a joke here. The entire world was baffled at the election results in 2000 in the United States. Our beacon of light was dimming quickly.

"It sounds like the recent elections in the United States, but we won't go there." The audience roared with laughter. Relieved the comic relief had worked, Jane continued after the audience had settled down.

"Regardless of how Anti-Decadent he was, Henley cannot completely separate himself from the Decadents, and indeed, as Henley's biographer, Jerome Hamilton Buckley points out, Henley and Wilde had great respect for each others' intellectual, poetic and artistic capabilities:

'Wilde, who lacked Henry James's high seriousness, was less likely to be silenced by an ironical rebuff. Yet he found it almost impossible to confute a Henleyan dictum; Henley he said at the end of his life, was the only man who ever had taxed to the full his intellect and ingenuity. This was high praise indeed to come for the artist in epigram. And Henley after Wilde's death returned the compliment; 'Wilde was clever,' he told Will Low – 'Clever? I should say he was. Seated where you are he has held the table against me, more than once.'

"Henley's poetry shows echoes of many French Symbolists and Decadents. His poetry uses free verse and relies on images of disease, death and decay to convey physical, spiritual and social demise. The French poet Mallarmé had a column in Henley's *National Observer* newspaper. Arthur Symons, at first a well-known Decadent poet and best known for his book *The Symbolist Movement in Literature* published in 1899, which led Eliot to read the French Symbolists, quoted Henley's poem 'Operation' completely in his article 'Mr. Henley's Poetry' published in 1892 in *Harper's New Monthly Magazine*. Symons also compared Henley to the French poet Verlaine in his 1893 article 'The Decadent Movement in Literature' in the *Fortnightly Review*. Symons wrote that the man's existence is concentrated into the example of the hospital, where a proximity of life and death is most obvious. This idea is also present in 'Operation', where even though the speaker is still alive, he already feels like a carcass while he is being carried to the operating theater. The effects of anesthesia on the speaker symbolize the limbo between life and death, which though here is most evident on the operating table, it is also constantly part of our existence, although we may not always choose to be aware of it.

You are carried in a basket
Like a carcase from the shambles,
To the theatre, a cockpit
Where they stretch you on a table.

Then they bid you close your eyelids
And they mask you with a napkin,
And the anaesthesic reaches
Hot and subtle through your being.

And you gasp and reel and shudder
In a rushing, swaying rapture,
While the voices at your elbow
Fade – receding – fainter – farther.

Lights about you shower and tumble,
And your blood seems crystallizing –
Edged and vibrant, yet within you
Racked and hurried back and forward."

The audience was silent. Beatrice Smith broke the silence with a poignant question that confirmed to Jane what she had hoped. Just as Jane had perceived Henley's "Operation" was alluded to in the first lines of Eliot's "Prufrock", where the night sky is spread out like patient anesthetized on a table, Jane sensed the same thought was on everyone else's mind and was echoing throughout the room.

"When is this from?" Beatrice Smith demanded.

"1873."

Dr. Lebenstein's prediction had come true. Walking through the city at rush hour on the way to an evening conference, Jane decided to ask another PhD student who was ten years younger than she was about an idea she had.

"Here's what I've been thinking about. Dante was on everyone's mind during the nineteenth century, and everyone in the nineteenth century equated the modern city with Dante's hell, especially because of the way cities expanded due to overpopulation. They just added another ring around the city every time they built another neighborhood. Time had also just been standardized because of the introduction of trains. Clocks could be seen everywhere in the city so that people could catch the train on time. Do you think that possibly the poets equated the turning of the clocks with the circles of Dante's hell?"

"Sure, why not?"

She wrote something up and sent it to Dr. Lebenstein and Dr. Ungaro. Dr. Ungaro sent it to Professor Stanford of her own accord.

> "Dear Dr. Lebenstein and Dr. Ungaro,
> I don't know whether this is far-fetched, but could you tell me whether it is something I should pursue? I've found a number of poems where I see similar echoes as in Eliot. What I've found is that the circling of the clock came to represent the circles of Dante's hell for the poets. Here are some examples of what I've found. It seems like it was a way to express their sense of man's inanity within the city landscape of the nineteenth century.
> Thank you in advance.
> Kind regards,
> Jane"

--------------------

From James Thomson's *The City of Dreadful Night*, 1880:
> He answered coldly, Take a watch, erase
> The signs and figures of the circling hours,
> Detach the hands, remove the dial-face:
> The works proceed until run down: although
> Bereft of purpose, void of use, still go.

From John Davidson "Railway Stations: London Bridge", 1909:
  Upon the delta wide of platforms, whence
  Discharges into London's sea, immense
  And turbulent, a brimming human flood,
  A river inexhaustible of blood
  [ …] And yet this human tide,
  As callous as the glaciers that glide
  A foot a day, but as a torrent swift,
  Sweeps unobservant save of time – for thrift
  Or dread disposes clockwards every glance –
  Right through a station which a seismic dance
  Chimerical alone can harmonize
  Even in imagination's friendly eyes.

In W.E. Henley's "London Voluntaries", 1893:
  And even the roar
  Of the strong streams of toil, that pause and pour
  Eastward and westward [...]
  [… … …]
  A tidal-race of lust from shore to shore
  [… … …]
  Since in the dim blue dawn of time
  The universal ebb-and-flow began [...]

From Henley again:
  'Tis time- 'tis time by his [*sic* Death's] ancient watch- to part
  From books and women and talk and drink and art.
  And you go humbly after him
  To a mean suburban lodging: on the way
  To what or where
  Not Death, who is old and very wise, can say:
  And you – how should you care
  So long as, unreclaimed of hell,
  The Wind-Fiend, the insufferable,
  Thus vicious and thus patient, sits him down
  To the black job of burking London Town?

From *The Waste Land*, T.S. Eliot, 1922:
  Unreal City,
  Under the brown fog of a winter dawn,

A crowd flowed over London Bridge, so many,
I had not thought death had undone so many.
Sighs, short and infrequent, were exhaled,
And each man fixed his eyes before his feet.
Flowed up the hill and down King William Street,
To where Saint Mary Woolnoth kept the hours
With a dead sound on the final stroke of nine.

From *The Waste Land,* T.S Eliot, 1922:
> At the violet hour, when the eyes and back
> Turn upward from the desk, when the human engine waits
> Like a taxi throbbing waiting,
> [… … …]
> At the violet hour, the evening hour that strives
> Homeward, and brings the sailor home from sea […].

Shortly after Jane sent this to her advisors, she had to call Dr. Lebenstein and Dr. Ungaro to set up another appointment before Christmas. At the end of the conversation, Dr. Lebenstein gave her some advice that was totally out of character, "Even if you don't get the money for your research again, don't give up. You've really got something here."

At their next appointment and after they had discussed the short piece she had written, Jane told Dr. Ungaro and Dr. Lebenstein she was three months pregnant. Dr. Lebenstein, who would not look up while she spoke and proceeded to straighten up his papers in order to leave, promptly dropped everything from where he was sitting as soon as the word "pregnant" crossed her lips. Dr. Ungaro tried to act like nothing had happened and congratulated her.

A few weeks later, Dr. Lebenstein made a comment about another pregnant woman's child that for some reason sent chills down her spine.

He said he hoped the child's eyes weren't crystal blue like his.

Unfortunately for Jane, this eerie prediction also came true despite the fact that she and her husband both had dark brown eyes.

ff

17 April 2001

Correspondence:    3 Queen Square      T 020 7465 0045         Faber and Faber Ltd
                   London             F 020 7465 0034         Publishers
                   WC1N 3AU           http://www.faber.co.uk

Matthew Evans
John Bodley
Walter Donohue
Valerie Eliot
Toby Faber
Laurence Longe
Julian Loose
Chris McLaren
Joanna Mackle
Jon Riley
Peter Simpson

Dear Ms ▇▇▇▇

Thank you for your letter of 27 March. I wonder if you could be a little more concise as to which of T.S. Eliot's manuscripts you wish to consult. Do you wish to quote from them?

Yours sincerely

Valerie Eliot

Registered Office
as above
Registered Number
944703

Valerie Eliot, Eliot's widow who he had married in his twilight years and was nearly thirty-eight years younger than he was, had replied to Jane's letter within a few weeks. Jane was surprised she had replied at all because of her elusive reputation among Eliot scholars. Mrs. Eliot had given Beatrice Smith permission to see Eliot's manuscripts after Beatrice Smith had met her at a conference, so Jane had mentioned Beatrice in her letter to Mrs. Eliot. Jane also mentioned that she was researching the connection between the late-nineteenth century British poets and Eliot and Pound. In the end, Jane didn't think that helped her with her request.

"17 April 2001

Dear Ms Sweens
Thank you for your letter of 27 March. I wonder if you could be a little more concise as to which of T.S. Eliot's manuscripts you wish to consult. Do you wish to quote from them?
Yours sincerely
Valerie Eliot"

Jane wrote her back and told Mrs. Eliot exactly what she wanted to see. Jane also explained that, at this time, she did not wish to quote from anything unless she required it for her research. Jane never heard from Mrs. Eliot again. She was not surprised by Mrs. Eliot's aloofness.

Dr. Lebenstein and Dr. Ungaro laughed at Mrs. Eliot's wide signature. So did Jane. It extended almost across the whole page. The "l" in Valerie made a slight rise and then dropped before it curved up again reaching across the page to the "e" that followed it.

Jane applied for a grant to go to Pound's archives at the Beinecke Rare Book and Manuscript Library at Yale. Jane had a hunch she could not put to rest: that if you can't get to one poet, you go through another, and that the way to Eliot was through Pound.

Professor Stanford helped Jane get accepted to a book. Three papers were accepted at three different conferences that fall. Professor Stanford was running two of them. She and Professor Stanford had also applied for financing of her PhD at the faculty for a second time after the first application had been turned down. This time, she had two recommendations from abroad; one from the US and one from a former tutor at Manchester, a man who had also tutored Dr. Ungaro and Beatrice Smith. Academia is small world indeed.

Then the night before she was supposed to read Eliot's "Preludes" at a poetry reading run by Dr. Rochdale and the rest of the English department, she went into premature labor, with Jane and her first daughter, Lisa, just barely surviving the delivery. During the most desperate moments for Jane and her baby, Jane's husband would disappear for a cigarette or a hamburger and not come back for hours. This was a week before her interview at the faculty.

For a second time, she was refused funding. A student who had half a grade point average higher than she did, but nothing else, got the money. The next time she saw Professor Stanford, his disappointment was palpable.

"Do you think we should try again?"

"No." The talkative American had seemingly taken on Dr. Rochdale's Oxbridge curtness. If she hadn't known him as long as she had, she might have misinterpreted his disappointment for academic arrogance. Recognizing the same despondence in CEOs right before they announced they were leaving the company, she decided to come right out and ask him.

"Are you looking for another professorship somewhere else?"

"Yes."

"Can I transfer my PhD to your new university?"

"Yes."

It was at dinner after the first day of the conference that Jane saw a very light-haired man sitting at the long university club dinner table. Seated in the middle and alone, turned around and smiling, obviously hoping for someone to arrive, she decided to sit down next to him. His very blond hair hid his age, and Jane thought he was a PhD student or a young scholar. He was Leif Leifson, a Norwegian and one of the top Modernist scholars in the world. He was chairing the conference with Professor Stanford and he had accepted Jane's article for the book on Modernism he was editing.

He and Jane enjoyed lively conversation all evening. Jane assumed that many there that evening thought she had sat there strategically. Envy and the benefit of the doubt do not rhyme, especially in scholarly circles.

The next day Jane gave her paper in the lecture hall where as a student she had always dreamed of delivering a lecture. Though she was far from being a lecturer yet, today was the day she made her mark in more ways than she could ever imagine.

Professor Stanford asked Jane whether she could present her paper a half hour ahead of time. That would give him a chance to test the visual equipment for the Modernist web of connections she had created and the Whistler paintings she had connected to Pound's poetry. Of course, she agreed, but felt sad because she knew Beatrice would miss her paper at the conference which she had promised to attend. A few days beforehand, she and Jane had had a spirited debate about Eliot. Because Beatrice loved Eliot so much, she had accused Jane of poetical patricide and suggested Jane look into some minor women poets for a change. Jane gave her the answer that Beatrice Smith's generation had longed to voice, but just didn't have the balls to say.

"I play with the big boys or I don't play at all."

Beatrice laughed and promised to come and hear Jane's paper. Dr. Lebenstein and Dr. Ungaro said nothing about attending, which made Beatrice's presence all the more important to Jane. It's better not to be alone in the lions' den.

Leif Leifson sat in the center of the lecture hall. The entire committee who had turned Jane down for financing sat next to each other in the second row. Her advisor sat to the far left end of the lecture hall and faced them as Jane did.

Professor Stanford introduced her and her subject and she read her paper.

* * *

## RETHINKING MODERNISM: ELIOT, POUND AND THE LATE-NINETEENTH CENTURY BRITISH POETS

This paper questions the periodization of Modernism in English-language poetry on the basis of an intertextual study into the work of the late-nineteenth century British poets James Thomson, Arthur Symons, John Davidson, W.E. Henley, and the early poetry of the Modernists T.S. Eliot and Ezra Pound. In this case study, I examine the validity of Eliot's and Pound's so-called break with their immediate literary predecessors such as the late-nineteenth century British poets, and I question their preference for associating themselves with canonical poets such as Baudelaire and Dante. This investigation is consistent with other recent works that discuss the canonical revision of Modernism such as Bonnie Kime Scott's *Refiguring Modernism* published in 1995. This paper demonstrates that Eliot's and Pound's early works were part of a system of poetics that already existed in late-nineteenth century British poetry before Eliot and Pound began writing.

Throughout their lives, Eliot and Pound made a number of inconsistent comments on their connection with the British poets, whose complete works have been out of print since the early twentieth century. Shortly before his death, and after years of speculation by literary critics, Eliot in three different sources disclosed that he had read the British poets between the ages of sixteen and twenty, so well before 1908, when he read the French Symbolists, and 1910, the year in which he discovered Dante. It is plausible, then, that Eliot's reading of the British poets predisposed his reading of the French Symbolists and of Dante, and co-conditioned his writing of *Prufrock and Other Observations* during this same period. Eliot also gave a series of lectures on the late-nineteenth century British poets and the French Symbolists between 1916 and 1919. To prepare for these lectures, he reread the British and French poets. During this same period Eliot wrote the collection *Poems*, published in 1920, and prepared to write *The Waste Land* published in 1922.

In a number of articles Pound published early in his career, he lauded the British poets for the innovations the latter had introduced into English poetry. Curiously, Pound did not have these articles included in his collected works. Still, many of the innovations figured in Pound's manifesto *Make It New* published in 1934. Equally curious, and in direct opposition to what he had argued in his early articles, with his poems "The Decadence" and *Hugh Selwyn Mauberley*, published in 1920, Pound actually contributed to the idea that the late-nineteenth century British poets had been literary failures.

Despite their inconsistency, Eliot's and Pound's early poetry up until the early 1920s can no longer be viewed as separate from the minor British works that preceded it. The British poets relied on the technique of borrowing, transposing and transforming texts from nineteenth-century French poetry, eighteenth-century urban English poetry, medieval Italian and English poetry, the Bible, Presbyterian hymnals, the critical works of Walter Pater, popular performances in London and Parisian music halls and modern urban scenes in paintings by James MacNeill Whistler to create a poetics of human existence in the modern city in their poetry. This pattern of borrowing, transposing and then transforming from the same texts likewise appears in the Modernist poetry of Eliot and Pound. Furthermore, the innovative poetic strategies most commonly associated with Eliot's and Pound's Modernist poetry, such as the use of personae in a modern urban setting and collage, are also integral to late-nineteenth century British poetry. Curiously, many literary critics see these poetic strategies as examples of how late-nineteenth century British poetry represented the fragmentation and decline of civilization. In contrast, these same poetic strategies are viewed as examples of how Eliot and Pound imposed order in their works based on literary tradition in a reaction to the chaotic fragmentation of society and culture around them. Yet, in essence, Eliot's and Pound's poetics are an extension of the British poetics that preceded them. Today I will present some evidence of the British web that Eliot and Pound belong to, or alternatively, the Modernist web the British poets belong to.

This web is based on biographical information, common poetic and artistic interests, similarities in their poetry and any criticism or passing comments that the poets wrote about any of the other poets. The next web shows the same connections, but the connections I will be discussing today are highlighted.

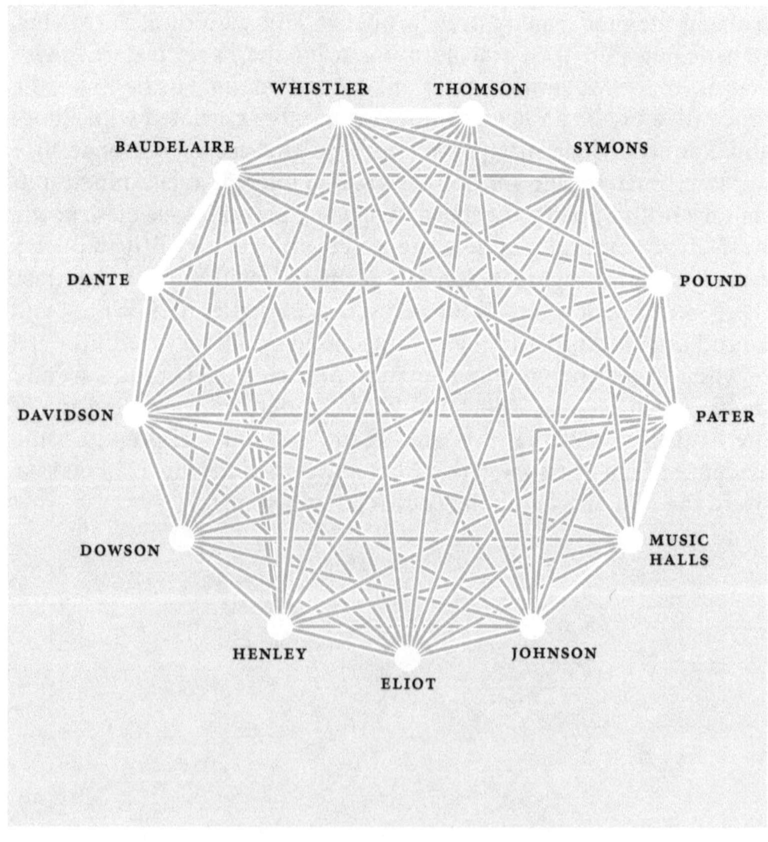

Here is the same web with Pound's connections in blue and Eliot's connections in red.

First I will examine Pound's connection to Pater, Whistler and the Decadent poet Arthur Symons. Secondly, I will examine Eliot's connection to the British poets James Thomson, John Davidson and W.E. Henley. Furthermore, I will demonstrate their connection to Dante, Baudelaire and Eliot.

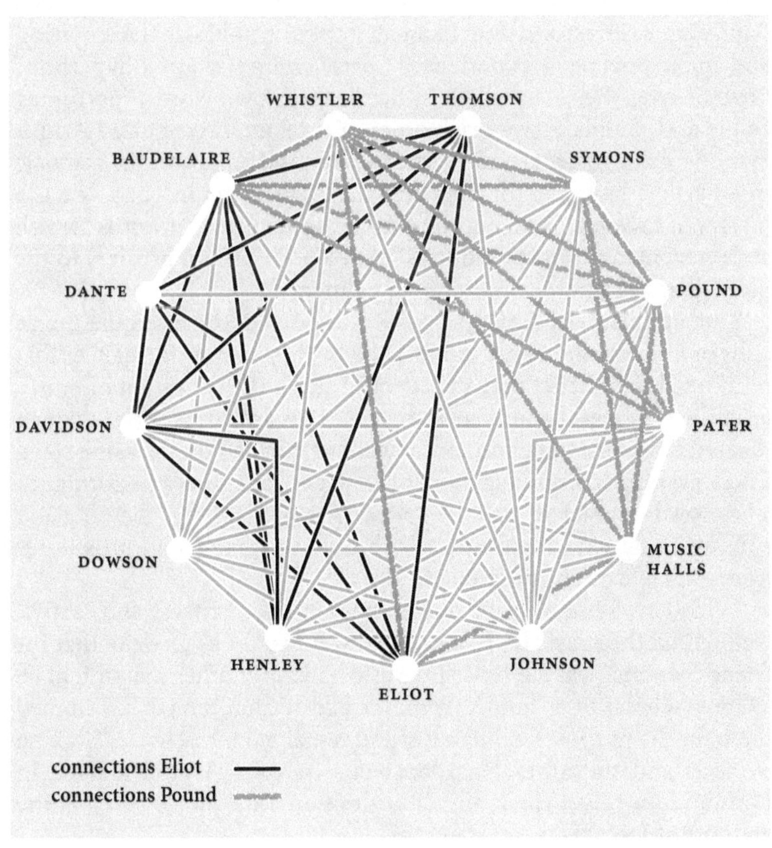

The aesthetics of symbolism constitute the most important links in the Pater-Baudelaire-Symons-Music Halls-Pound web that in the end would be crucial to Pound's ideas of Imagism. In that symbolist web, music and synesthesia play an important role. Like Baudelaire, who prescribed that poetry "should be musical, but lacking rhyme and rhythm", the British poets and Eliot and Pound tried to incorporate musicality in their verse. Moreover, they followed Walter Pater's belief that "all art aspires to the condition of music". The artists and poets of the time considered music the only art in which form and content are inseparable, and one of the aesthetics of the time prescribed that all the arts should be synthesized with music so that their art could attain the condition of music.

At the same time, many poets, and especially Symons, applied Baudelaire's *correspondances* in an attempt to emphasize the empirical and make poetry an experience. *Correspondances* are a hyperbolic form of synesthesia, in which in Baudelaire's own words, "perfumes, colors and sounds answer each other". Ezra Pound recognized Arthur Symons' achievement to unify the literary, the optic and the acoustic in an article he wrote for the periodical *Atheneum* in 1920, "he is a master of cadence…or a new modus in the sequence of words" which as "a new manner of speech is as great a boon (if not greater) to the intelligence as a new colour among painters".

During this period, many artists and poets frequented the music halls of London and Paris. In music halls, they saw performances that reinforced their belief that all art could attain the condition of music, or at the very least be unified with it. Various art forms such as dance, theater, tableau vivant, and music were performed on the same stage. These evenings constituted more of an experience than a performance. The crowd interacted with the performers by clapping, cheering and singing along with the music, alcohol flowed freely and prostitutes were available on the promenade.

Whistler, Symons and the other poets, writers and artists frequented the music halls, and Yeats went so far as to write that his friend Symons "was a scholar in music halls as another man might be a Greek scholar or an authority on the age of Chaucer. He has studied them for the purposes of literature and remained himself […]". Taking Symons and the other Decadents cue in 1908, Pound arrived in London in a velvet cloak and later donned a turquoise earring, the epitome of Decadence.

During his stays in London and Paris, he witnessed the rapid demise of the music halls at the hands of the cinema. For the astute Pound, this was further proof the modern world would be an increasingly visual one, and its inhabitants would be conditioned by images much more than sound. Pound said of the city, "Life of the village is narrative [...] In a city visual impressions succeed each other, overlap, overcross, they are cinematographic". Though musical rhythm in poetry was important, the emphasis must be on the image. So between Pater, Whistler, the late-nineteenth century British poets, and Pound, there is an unmistakable popular connection to each of their work that takes its form in the music hall.

But how were synesthesia and music incorporated into the work of these artists to create an experience? Whistler, who was an important role model for Eliot and Pound as an American artist in Europe, used music in combination with color to point to the connection between his work and music. The result are a number of urban landscapes with musical titles, but also portraits with musical titles such as "Symphony 1,2 and 3 in White", all painted in the 1860s. Symphony 1 and 2 also have the additional subtitles "The White Girl", and I have three overheads to show you now.

Keeping the musical titles in mind, notice the softness the paintings radiate and that the women are essentially one with the color white. And also take note of the flowers, especially the lily in the first painting.

Arthur Symons uses similar images in his poem "Morbidezza", published in 1896, which is the Italian for "soft". In this poem, Symons uses Baudelaire's *correspondances* which fuses images, sounds, scents and the tactile together in order to render the poem into an experience.

> White Girl, your flesh is lilies,
> Grown 'neath a frozen moon,
> So still is
> The rapture of your swoon
> Of whiteness, snow or lilies.
>
> The virginal revealment,
> Your bosom's wavering slope,
> Concealment,
> 'Neath fainting heliotrope,
> O whitest white's revealment

*James Whistler, Symphony in White, No. 1: The White Girl. 1862.*
*National Gallery of Art, Washington D.C.*

*James Whistler, Symphony in White, No. 2: The Little White Girl. 1864.
Tate Gallery, London.*

James Whistler, *Symphony in White, No. 3. 1865–67.*
*The Barber Institute of Fine Arts, The University of Birmingham.*

Is like a bed of lilies,
A jealous-guarded row,
Whose will is
Simply chaste dreams: – but oh,
The alluring scent of lilies!

In "Morbidezza", the vision of the girl becomes a symbolist experience in a "unification of sensibility" as Eliot once said. Her whiteness is not part of her, but it is her, and the speaker even remarks that her flesh is lilies, and in a simile, compares the revelation of her flesh to a bed of lilies. The heliotrope she wears is as inherent to her as the scent of lilies are to lilies themselves, so the two objects become conflated into one. Symons also elaborates on the various hues of white he sees: there is the white of the girl's flesh, the whiteness of the lilies and snow, the symbolic "whiteness" of "chaste dreams". Furthermore, "Morbidezza" is written in a simple song-like ABABA rhyme scheme, a technique often used by late-nineteenth century British poets in order to attempt to unify their poetry with music.

In Pound's Imagist poem "Alba", we can see the connections to Whistler and Symons's work, where the girl beside him is compared in a simile to lilies:

As cool as the pale wet leaves
of the lily-of-the-valley
She lay beside me in the dawn.

In "Alba", which is the Italian for "dawn", we can see as late as 1913 Pound's connection to Symons and Whistler. The title "Alba" echoes Symons and many other poets' interest in literatures other than English, and the late-nineteenth century predilection for poetry at moments of dawn or twilight, moments in the day which allowed variations in color because of the variances in light. Here Pound echoes Whistler's and Symons' hues of white, there is the whiteness of the flesh, the pallor of the leaves, and the whiteness that is the lily-of-the-valley. Pound also echoes the synesthesia with "cool" and "wet". Finally, the poem is musical in that it strives to unify content and form through the simile and in the particular rhythm of the words. However, much more than in Symons, the emphasis of the poem lies in its visual aspects, and not in imagery, but in images.

Inanity is a recurrent theme in the poetry of James Thomson, John Davidson, W.E. Henley and T.S. Eliot that stems from late-nineteenth century mood poetry in which feelings of ennui and listlessness were expounded upon. Thomson, Davidson, Henley and Eliot deal primarily with the collective inanity of mankind. The poets' source for images is Dante's *Inferno*, where the damned are condemned to wandering perpetually round and round in the circles of hell and poets are stuck in a useless existence in the First Circle Hell, or Limbo. In the poetry of Thomson, Davidson, Henley and Eliot, the circular walls of Dante's *Inferno* are replaced by the circling of the clock, for it is time that controls the modern city-dwellers lives. The perpetual wanderings of the condemned in Dante recur in James Thomson's *The City of Dreadful Night*, published in 1880, where the inhabitants of the city wander without purpose, and are especially poignant in the section where a man perpetually makes a pilgrimage to the three shrines of dead Faith, dead Love and dead Hope. The shrines are situated in such a way that he can only reach the next shrine by turning right, and thus in a constant circular motion. The speaker of *The City of Dreadful Night* then asks the man whether life is viable and how it can continue if Faith, Love and Hope are dead. The man in Thomson's poem answers the speaker allegorically by using a clock without hands, dial or face as a symbol for the inanity of man's life; even without the purpose of telling time, the clock still ticks, much like man who, even without meaning or purpose continues to move through his daily routine:

> He answered coldly, Take a watch, erase
> The signs and figures of the circling hours,
> Detach the hands, remove the dial-face:
> The works proceed until run down: although
> Bereft of purpose, void of use, still go.

John Davidson presents the image in "Railway Stations: London Bridge", published in 1909, of the masses being enslaved to the clock. The masses resemble Dante's condemned or Baudelairean phantoms more than human beings, and this image of the living dead emphasizes the horror behind the speaker's realization of mankind's inanity.

Upon the delta wide of platforms, whence
Discharges into London's sea, immense
And turbulent, a brimming human flood,
A river inexhaustible of blood
[ …] And yet this human tide,
As callous as the glaciers that glide
A foot a day, but as a torrent swift,
Sweeps unobservant save of time – for thrift
Or dread disposes clockwards every glance -
Right through a station which a seismic dance
Chimerical alone can harmonize
Even in imagination's friendly eyes.

In W.E. Henley's "London Voluntaries", published in 1893, time is repeatedly shown to control the daily routine of the Londoners. The poem starts by describing the bells of St. Margaret's, and later St. Paul's, ringing out omnisciently over the rest of the city. The sound of hordes of commuters traveling home at the end of the workday also appears in "London Voluntaries".

And even the roar
Of the strong streams of toil, that pause and pour
Eastward and westward [...]
[... ... ...]
A tidal-race of lust from shore to shore
[... ... ...]
Since in the dim blue dawn of time
The universal ebb-and-flow began [...]

In Henley, even the actions of the phantasmagoric figure Death are controlled by time, and more specifically, a watch. Echoing Davidson's text, Death travels home with a commuter, also a new phenomenon for the late-nineteenth century urbanite. Emphasizing the commuter's inane existence and echoing Thomson's pilgrim, Death cannot tell the commuter what the purpose of his existence is. Uncaring and dehumanized by the silent realization of his inanity, the commuter carries on his daily routine apathetic to the filth and disease of his community:

'Tis time – 'tis time by his ancient watch – to part
From books and women and talk and drink and art.
And you go humbly after him
To a mean suburban lodging: on the way
To what or where
Not Death, who is old and very wise, can say:
And you – how should you care
So long as, unreclaimed of hell,
The Wind-Fiend, the insufferable,
Thus vicious and thus patient, sits him down
To the black job of burking London Town?

In Eliot's *The Waste Land*, the speakers use allusions to Dante and echoes of Thomson, Davidson and Henley to describe the crowds and to depict how the Londoners' daily routine is controlled by time, and more specifically, the circling of the clock. The speaker alludes to Dante's *Inferno* where Pilgrim states, "and behind it came so long a train of people / that I should never have believed death had / undone so many". Ghostly, nameless and unfeeling, Eliot's crowd flows over London Bridge as easily as the filthy Thames underneath it. The speaker implicitly compares the movement of the crowd to a river, as Davidson's crowd was implicitly compared to the currents of a river, and Henley's crowd was compared to the tides. The bells of Henley's St. Margaret's and St. Paul's ringing omnisciently over the Londoners resurfaces in Eliot. The crowd in Eliot flows toward the sound of Saint Mary Woolnoth keeping the hours as if they are on a pilgrimage, like the lone figure in Thomson's *The City of Dreadful Night*:

Unreal City,
Under the brown fog of a winter dawn,
A crowd flowed over London Bridge, so many,
I had not thought death had undone so many.
Sighs, short and infrequent, were exhaled,
And each man fixed his eyes before his feet.
Flowed up the hill and down King William Street,
To where Saint Mary Woolnoth kept the hours
With a dead sound on the final stroke of nine.

In *The Waste Land*, the speaker reiterates the image of London's inhabitants being controlled by time. As in Henley's "London Voluntaries" where the speaker announces "lo! the Wizard Hour!", Eliot's speaker announces "the violet hour" that releases the next hordes of city dwellers. Davidson's "Railway Stations: London Bridge" is echoed, too, where every glance is turned clockwards.

> At the violet hour, when the eyes and back
> Turn upward from the desk, when the human engine waits
> Like a taxi throbbing waiting,
> [... ... ...]
> At the violet hour, the evening hour that strives
> Homeward, and brings the sailor home from sea [...].

To conclude, it is obvious from these texts that Eliot and Pound did indeed look to the world around them and to literary tradition for the inspiration for their work. However, their immediate predecessors did also, and they did it successfully. Although many of these poets' complete works have been out of print since the early twentieth century, there are many echoes of these poets in the work of Eliot and Pound. These findings therefore do warrant a questioning of the periodization of Modernism in English-language poetry, for if anything, it removes Eliot's and Pound's exclusive rights to Modernism.

* * *

A complete silence fell over the lecture hall. Leif Leifson broke it.

"This is fascinating."

Jane smiled and thanked him. The committee would not raise their eyes. Jane shot a glance at Professor Stanford. He was beaming.

A professor from London and good friend of Professor Stanford, who Jane had had a beer with once, asked her whether she could elaborate.

A bit stunned, she asked, "Is there anything particular you would like me to elaborate on?"

"Based on what you've found so far, what comes to mind?"

"Well, one thing I've been thinking about lately is how three-dimensional the connections in the web are. Almost like geometric planes that intersect perpendicularly. I can only show you how the poets and artists are connected two-dimensionally because that's the only medium I have right now. But there are so many connections in the poetry, the art world and society before Eliot and Pound started writing, and that foundation was already there for them to build upon."

Beatrice walked in and sat down.

There was another hush.

Professor Stanford decided that it was time for a coffee break and the scholars quickly poured out of the lecture hall. As Jane straightened up her papers, the professor from London hurried up to her in a flustered excitement, "Jane, it's fascinating to see where this dissertation is going. Good work."

Now alone, Jane left the lecture hall. Standing outside the lecture hall, all but one of the professors turned their back on her as if trying to avoid a contagious disease. One woman professor walked up to her, though obviously embarrassed because she dared risk the scorn of her peers, and offered Jane a piece of paper with a title and author's name on it.

"You need to take a look at this." She handed it to Jane awkwardly and walked away. Again Jane stood there alone, unfinanced, untitled and totally unaware of what she had unleashed.

Word had spread to the English department and the other literature departments by the afternoon. Dr. Lebenstein suddenly showed up for the afternoon session but did not acknowledge Jane. He walked past her and acted as if she didn't exist. The head of the financing committee and professor of comparative literature had the afternoon chair not only announce him, but all of his books, too. Carbuncular and childless, the only professor Jane had ever known who wore T-shirts and worked out in a gym, he was the epitome of the hedonism of his generation. Having married his much older PhD advisor, herself a ubiquitous dinosaur among the theorists who had come out of the 1960s and '70s, his very presence reeked of an Oedipal smell. Dr. Lebenstein despised him, but could not say anything because in the pecking order that existed, he was only a doctor. Lucky for all attending, the professor from London despised the comparative literature professor even more and challenged every aspect of his argument. It was obvious to the professor from London and all others present that the comparative literature professor made general assumptions without knowing any of his texts.

Jane had decided at the coffee break that the best way to get through the rest of the conference and to promote her survival in general was to keep her mouth shut and let them fight it out amongst themselves.

It was Dr. Rochdale's retirement reception and he was in good spirits. When it was Jane's turn to shake his hand and offer him her small gift, he bellowed joyously, "Where is your infant? What's her name?"

"Lisa."

"Weren't you supposed to read 'Preludes' at the Eliot poetry reading?" Jane had heard that he and her other tutors had bragged about how well she had read Henley's "Operation".

"Yes, I was, but I went into labor prematurely that night."

"Oh." He paused, embarrassed, but then seized the opportunity to let his English wit shine through. "You were zapped by the ghost of Eliot!" He bellowed and they both roared with laughter.

You had to respect English wit, Jane thought. It was all in the timing.

Jane's whole family had flown over for Lisa's baptism. They were all in a celebratory mood despite the animosity between her parents and especially between her mother and her father's new wife. When she and her father were alone and she was the in kitchen sterilizing baby bottles, Jane asked her dad why he had never told them he was delivered by William Carlos Williams.

"Why didn't you ever tell us you were delivered by William Carlos Williams? That's so amazing, Dad." Jane was totally unprepared for his response.

He turned around and glared at Jane with eyes of shock, "How did you find out?"

Startled by the vehemence of her father's response, Jane answered demurely. "Mom told me. Grandma told her."

Neither of them dared utter a single word.

Jane was seriously considering giving up. Professor Stanford regained his enthusiasm again, though he continued to look for another professorship, and advised her to apply for financing from the faculty for a third time. Then he was diagnosed with cancer. To set her mind on other sights, she managed to get a job in the higher echelons of a Dutch bank. But when her boss started opening her mail and the secretary was demoted because she was pregnant, Jane knew being a mother would not help her. When her boss questioned why she couldn't stay until 9:00 pm like everyone else in the company, Jane told her because daycare closed at 6:30 pm.

Then her boss asked, "Well, what will they do? Put your children on the street?"

"No, I'll get fined and I can't bring her the next day."

"A fine, that's it? Can't you just pay it?"

"But then I can't bring her the next day."

Jane knew she was not going to convince her. Her days were numbered there. Jane got fired the following Monday, and her boss let one of her puppets tell Jane instead of telling her herself.

The day she realized she was about to be fired, Jane sat despondent in the train staring at the lush, green fields around her and longed for the joy of spring. Now, all she could think about was how to pay for childcare until she found another job. She did not want to be stuck at home again, isolated with only the occasional appointment at the department to sustain her socially. Whatever happened, Professor Stanford had to get better first. Dr. Lebenstein and Dr. Ungaro had to take over his classes, so she wouldn't be seeing them for awhile either because they were too busy.

When she got home, a letter had arrived from a foundation she had applied to almost a year earlier. She had totally forgotten about it. It was the only foundation in the Netherlands that supported women who were writing their PhDs without any funding. She opened it without expecting much and read the first line, "It is our pleasure to inform you…"

"Oh my God, I got the money! Yes!"

"What's going on?" her husband asked.

"I got the grant to go to the Beinecke Rare Book and Manuscript Library to see Pound's archives at Yale. I can't believe it. We're going to Yale! We have to take Lisa with us! We can say she went to Yale!"

"Why do want to do that PhD anyway? The only thing those poets talk about is death and all I see at university receptions are old men in gray suits. Why do you want to hang out with a bunch of gray suits?"

Jane celebrated that night with her daughter who was now nearly one year old.

As Jane sat there in the glass-walled reading room in the Beinecke at Yale, she realized that different realities really did exist solely because of money. The glass walls of the reading room allowed the librarians to watch the readers with hawks' eyes, like the librarian who had sized Jane up in Amsterdam.

Though they were clearly watching the readers, they hid it courteously. The librarians were busy as bees processing all folder and box requests which they communicated back to the assistants in the archives with walky-talkies lest one second of precious scholarly time be wasted.

If the pressure got to be too much for the scholars, or, heaven forbid, one of their requests would need extra time to process, they could always take a rest and order a refreshment in the Beinecke lounge just outside the reading room and adjacent to the librarians' counter. Complete with Persian rugs, oak paneling and a portrait of the philanthropic industrialist, it was obvious that the maintenance of the lounge alone took a big chunk of out the industrialist's taxable income.

But that was beside the point, Jane thought. If people like him didn't establish and fund these places, where would our cultural heritage go? Knowing that European universities would discard a collection at the drop of a hat if policy dictated them to do so, though being run by the state and having ministers of culture, Jane thought it wasn't such a bad idea that an industrialist should have a manuscript library named after him. Leave culture to the wealthy industrialists who understand the mechanics of long-term policy and the need to invest in the future, she thought. At least they understand that our cultural heritage must outlive them and belongs to posterity.

The librarian called her. The first box had arrived from the archives. She collected the box and sat down in the reading room. She was pregnant with her second child and it felt good to sit down and get down to work. Here was something already. Pound and Symons had published regularly in the *Fortnightly Review* between 1914–1918. That meant that Symons had not completely disappeared from the literary scene. Interesting.

She returned the box and waited for the second one. In it were letters from John Quinn.

She prodded her memory. "John Quinn? Wasn't that the lawyer who had *The Waste Land* manuscripts?" She thought to herself. Looking at the letter, she realized that was not the only manuscript Quinn was interested in. Pound had criticized American collectors in a magazine in January 1915 and questioned whether they knew the cultural value, not just the monetary value, of what they were buying.

Quinn was quick to defend himself in a letter dated February 25, 1915.

"Two years ago I sold all of my Meredith, Morris, Swinburne, Henley and other manuscripts. I bought the Henley manuscripts and then sold them for the same price plus the cost of making solander cases for them."

In another letter to Pound dated March 24, 1916, Quinn boasts about spending £50 on Symons. "Why was he buying all of these manuscripts?" she thought to herself. Henley and Symons were hardly heard of anymore by that time. She took some notes and returned the box.

The next box arrived. More vanilla folders and more letters. Then one folder caught her eye with the name "T.S. Eliot" on it. She pulled it from the box and slowly opened it. The letters were ordered chronologically and she looked down at them and stared. These were T.S. Eliot's letters to Ezra Pound. She turned one after the other and scanned the dates: 1915, 1917, 1919, 1922. Eliot's letters up until 1922 had already been published. But the pile of letters continued: 1924, 1925, 1927, 1928, 1929…. Jane quickly fingered through the top right-hand corners of the letters, skimming through the dates in front of her. The letters continued until November 17, 1939, just after the outbreak of the Second World War. These were Eliot's unpublished letters to Pound.

Her heart pounded. The baby kicked. She remained hunched over the letters, but looked up to see what the librarians were doing. Everyone was going about their work. At least for them, it was business as usual.

At the Houghton at Harvard, if they discovered you were looking at Eliot's unpublished work but didn't have written permission from Mrs. Eliot, they would snatch it from under your eyes. It had happened to a few scholars, and only increased everyone's intrigue. Jane decided to look at the letters as much as she could and take as many notes as she could before she returned the box and confessed she did not have permission to see them.

Then she started thinking naughty. Maybe I could steal them, she thought. No, I'd never get them out of the library. I'd be arrested and I'd never be able to come back again or visit any other libraries. No, take as many notes as you can and then try honesty. Honesty is the best policy.

She wrote pages of notes and went quickly through one letter after the other. The tone changed after 1922. There were promises; promises of publications, suggestions of collections, promises of lectures in America. But Jane knew nothing ever materialized. Pound wasn't really widely published until the 1970s and he lived penniless in Italy at the time. Then there were handwritten messages at the bottom of the Eliot's letters.

September 21, 1933: "Solicitors ARE expensive." Isn't that a threat? Jane thought. Weren't they friends?

Then in a letter dated 25 January 1934, Jane read what looked like another threat. "Podesta, the young & enterprising firm of Faber & Faber is forchnite in having secured the services of Mr. T.S. Eliot, at a salary named

(in milreis, lei etc.)

in five or six figgers/. After 12 years with the Federation of British Industries Mr. Eliot is probly better qualified than any other Big Executive to cope with the task for which he has been engaged, which is to superintend the department devoted to correspondence with Mr. Ezra Pound. In our rotogravure secture our readers will find to-day a portrait of the celebrated condottiere, beneath the palmettos of his native Rappaloo in conversation with Gen. Goering. This photograph, for the authenticity of which we vouch, will give our readers some idea of the magnitude of the job which Mr. Eliot has undertaken. When interviewed on the subject Mr. Eliot observed to our representative: 'I rose from nothing – and I stop at nothing.'"

And the insults. 2 October, 1935: "Dear Ez, Now look Here, les get ground to that problem of Selected essays again, and a very pretty little problem it is too. Touch 3/4ing the most fasces of faeces you just sent, that is very fruity little bit in the HOOT."

More threats were in the last letter dated 17 November 1939. "Resp. Ez, Referring to yours of 2nd instant. It is NOT clear. If it's that you want to Reprint those two abortive dialogue in a Periodical, or separately, or entire, that's no go: my juvenilia is only for publication after I have been dead too Long to be able to prevent it. If you cd. Help me to SURRPRESS much of what I have written, instead of tryin to resurrect what I have SURPRESSED, you would be bein Useful & Practical. Nobody can prevent you, I spose from Quotin' anything I ever said in order to PROVE how much more intelligent I used to be before I was took of the bottle and put onto gruel: but you may be assured that I will prevent Everything I CAN."

Jane got as much written down as she could and then took the folder to the librarian.

"Ma'am, I don't have permission to see this."

The librarian was a small, feisty African-American woman with the same resolve and audacity that would give hope back to the world a few years later. "We have our own laws here. Would you like me to make copies for you?"

Jane lay in the bed awake at the Duncan Hotel in New Haven in the middle of the night. Her husband ground his teeth while he slept, the sound of which was intolerable.

Lisa slept peacefully. The baby kicked in Jane's belly, aroused by Jane's rare nocturnal vigil.

It felt strangely stimulating to be in the hotel Dr. Lebenstein had recommended to her. The same hotel he had stayed at when he researched Pound's archives at Yale. The Duncan was a remnant of the early twentieth century and its manually-operated elevator built at that time was still in use.

Unfortunately, only members of the hotel staff were allowed to operate the elevator to avoid any accidents from happening.

Jane attended two of the string of farewell lunches and drinks that had been organized for Professor Stanford. Walking to one of the luncheons together with Professor Stanford, he revealed to her a loyalty that startled her.

"You do realize one of the reasons I resigned was how your PhD was handled."

Jane had no answer.

"Make sure you transfer your dissertation to my new university."

At the drinks she attended for Professor Stanford, Dr. Lebenstein ignored her the entire evening except at the end just when she, her husband and Lisa were heading out the door.

Dr. Lebenstein wanted to see what Lisa looked like. Jane's husband fumed at Dr. Lebenstein's presence.

Now well into her pregnancy with Danielle, Jane had at no other time in her life sensed how vulnerable she really was in what is still a man's world.

That summer Jane and her family exchanged houses with friends, an Italian and Dutch couple, she and her husband had met in Houston. Since Jane and her husband had moved back to the Netherlands, their friends had also moved back to Europe but they chose to return to Italy where he was from. He refused to live in the Netherlands for any long period of time ever again because of the weather and what he considered the lack of passion for life that was so prevalent there. She was Dutch and exchanging houses meant they could visit her family while whoever they exchanged houses with could borrow his parents' apartment in Rapallo on the coast. It was the perfect solution for a young family.

Jane had not touched her dissertation in ages. The care of two young children and no help from her husband drained most of her energy. He did nothing to help her maintain their social circles or help her stay in a job long term. Professor Stanford was gone and she had not yet completed the paperwork to transfer her dissertation. Dr. Lebenstein was caught up in messy divorce. Dr. Ungaro was suffering from heart trouble and neither tutor had been able to keep appointments with anyone for some time now. Consequently, Jane found very little to sustain her soul.

Then while walking to the store one morning in Rapallo, a marble sign with gold letters standing at the edge of a small square in the middle of town reminded her of what had sustained her for her entire life: poetry. The name of the square was the Giardino di Ezra Pound. During discussions with her friends regarding the details of the trip, so removed from her core had she gone astray, she had completely overlooked the fact that this was the same town in Italy where Eliot had addressed his letters to Pound, the copies of which still rested in her attic.

Pound had lived here for years. His restless presence reignited the dormant kindlings in her soul and made them glow again.

When her husband discovered the same square two days later and laughed at her in public, yelling, "You'll never get away from it, will you? HAHAHAHAHA!". And while they walked with their two daughters to try a different ice cream shop, the rekindling suddenly made her attune to his intolerable insults which she soon would accept no more.

One of the financing committee members, a professor of French, contacted Jane and asked for her address. He had a copy of the book he had just published on his desk with her article in it. He had kept a copy for her; an author's copy, he said.

It was a different project than Leif Leifson's, but with similar topics and published in Dutch. The French professor had asked her in February to contribute the paper she had presented at the conference in 2001. She tried to decline, stating health problems, work commitments and family obligations, but he persisted. So Jane agreed to contribute her paper, but could only submit it in English. Though Jane spoke and wrote Dutch so much like a native speaker that many did not believe her when she told them she was American, she did not trust the professor's intentions and told him that was all she could do at this time.

He responded with an offer from Dr. Lebenstein. Dr. Lebenstein would translate it for her. Dr. Lebenstein sent her his draft on Maundy Thursday and wished her a happy Easter.

April is the cruellest month, she thought, wondering whether it was all a sick joke. She read his draft and approved it without really looking at it on the day before Easter.

She had not bothered to read his translation of her original title, "Rethinking Modernism". Dr. Lebenstein had renamed her article to "A New Light on Modernism: Eliot, Pound and the Late-Nineteenth Century British Poets". Dr. Lebenstein, the professor of French and the chief editor who was also a famous Flemish poet and was based at the university where Professor Stanford had transferred to in Belgium, made sure her article was as high on the table of contents as university politics would allow. They got her in at chapter two, behind the childless and carbuncular comparative literature professor who would have it no other way than to be chapter one. The poet did not mention him in his introduction, but praised Jane's article wholeheartedly.

That summer in 2005, Dr. Lebenstein had accepted an award from the Ezra Pound Society at the conference they had held in Rapallo, a year after Jane had spent her summer there and Pound had nudged her out of her slumber.

Some people never get their timing right.

Three weeks after Jane received the book, she quit her part-time teaching job at a local school that had hired her because they believed native speakers of English would bring in more pupils. They told her it was a good job for a mother because it was part-time. But she, like the other native speakers, soon realized that was the only thing the school thought she was good for. Her husband was glad she quit and started talking about wanting a third child, something he had never wanted before.

She did not tell him that the reason she had quit her job was because she wanted to rethink her life. She decided it was safer to keep that to herself and immediately visited her family doctor so she could get back on the pill. A good family doctor is a girl's best friend.

Beatrice Smith was dead. Just five years after she had defended her PhD and just a year after her husband had divorced her when he discovered she was having an affair, she lay dead in a closed coffin to cover her body mangled with disease. She was too emaciated to be publicly shown, so voraciously had the tumors eaten away at her body, just as her husband's lack of attention for her had eaten away at her soul. Seeking solace in a lover, she found only more solitude when she was diagnosed with terminal cancer and her lover left her, and she died alone in a hospice.

Jane just happened to read the obituary in the newspaper two days after Christmas. Beatrice's cuckolded husband had only placed the obituary in the paper instead of sending invitations to the funeral, but the members of the English department found out by chance one by one after a few members saw the ad. The academics' insatiable need for salacious gossip took care of the rest and the whole department showed up for the funeral.

Jane sat in the church in disbelief listening to Beatrice's death knells tolling outside. What had happened? Where had time gone? What had happened to the life Beatrice had bursting inside of her?

Sitting in the church listening to the bells that summoned the mourners to the bereaved family, and especially Beatrice's grown children who were already seated, all Jane knew is that she could not let this happen to her.

"There's just something I need to do." Jane ran to the mailbox to mail the letter she had been meaning to send for years to her maternal great aunt. She didn't have to strain her ears to make out the impatient sighs and boorish grunts her husband and his family made while she walked twenty yards to the mailbox at the corner of her in-laws' street. They had waited hours for her in-laws to get ready, but that half a minute for Jane was just too much extra waiting to bear.

Her daughters looked on in silence.

After years of nagging that they should rent a house for the summer in France like they did year after year when her husband was a boy, Jane and her husband finally agreed to go on vacation with his parents. Jane looked forward to going to France, where she had once wanted to study politics. She had spent summer after summer studying French at the Sorbonne in order to speak as much like a Frenchwoman as she could. No American with a sense of history and grace could forget the effect Jacqueline Kennedy had on De Gaulle, even though it plunged the country into the war that changed us forever.

Jane could not remember how many times she had mentioned to her husband's parents that she had studied French at the Sorbonne in order to connect with them. Her husband's father was a French teacher and her husband's mother had been conditioned to like what his father liked. Even though Jane had not used her French to study politics, when she heeded her calling to literature, even English and American literature, her command of French had become indispensable. Especially when she studied the connections between the French Symbolists, the late-nineteenth century British poets and the Modernists.

Many times Jane had used her knowledge of French to try and start a conversation with her in-laws. This was something they had in common and for years she had extended her hand to try and find a commonality with them. Only it wasn't until they got to France she realized they had never listened.

Neither her husband nor his family had listened. Nothing, no response, silence, solitary confinement for fifteen years.

When they met the owners of the house they were renting from, her in-laws started talking with the owners and immediately translated the French for her so that she could understand. Dumbfounded, she realized they had not listened for all those years.

They had assumed and rested comfortably in the assumption that Jane was a dumb American. Jane decided to shake them out of their comfort zone.

After enduring their translations for a few minutes to let them bask in their presumed glory, Jane whipped out in perfect French how much she loved French cooking and was particularly interested in regional French cooking. She asked the owners if they could show her a few recipes native to the Corrèze?

Within ten minutes Jane was standing in the kitchen with one of the owners making ratatouille with vegetables from their garden. Word spread like wildfire in the village about "la belle Americaine" and within a few days Jane had the entire village at her feet. When she went running in the morning, the villagers out on their balconies would raise their fists and cheer her on and call her "la courageuse".

Her husband's parents were green with envy. A Dutch expression said that they were so envious, they would drink her blood. Jane realized that had they had the chance, they would have.

A few days after their arrival, Jane sat in the garden and watched how her father-in-law called his wife every thirty seconds to find out where she was. As Jane watched her mother-in-law rush back and forth between his callings with her gray complexion, cheeks sunken and shallow from lack of life, and her body emaciated from never having time to eat because her husband always demanded his wife attend to his needs immediately, Jane realized that she had to get out of this now or end up like her.

Jane and her family and in-laws were nearing the end of their stay in the Corrèze. The meteor showers of early August were about to take place and Jane decided to wake her children up at 3:00 am so that they could watch the shower together under the sky that could shine uninhibited from any city lights nearby.

Her in-laws protested voraciously that she should wake two children up at 3:00 am, three and five years old, and go lay down on the cold ground with them to watch a meteor shower, but Jane had decided not to listen to anything or anyone else anymore except her own heart.

She had a hunch that just as she had seen the Norwegian sun above the fjords around midsummer and understood why Munch had painted the sun the way he did, that perhaps seeing the stars at night here in the French countryside would help her understand why Van Gogh had painted *Starry Night* the way he did. She wanted to share that with her daughters.

Lying on blankets to protect them from the wetness of the dew and under blankets to protect them from the crisp but refreshing cold night air that they breathed in deeply, Jane and her daughters, Lisa and Danielle, gazed at the orchestra of shooting and spinning stars above. One after the other, the stars fell to the earth while those that remained in the sky radiated so brightly, they seemed to be spinning in a vortex.

And Jane and her daughters understood Van Gogh.

A letter was waiting for Jane when she got home. It was from her great aunt and it contained more history in it than she could ever have imagined.

"Dear Jane,
Your letter was a delight to know you wanted 'Family History'. The best research was done by Carl and Emma Cobaugh. He retired from AT&T. P.O. Box 729, Waynesburg, PA 15370–0729. In reference to your request in your letter of July 22, 2006 – I am setting forth the following: this portion of the Sensheshin Family History covering the immigration of the family to America commences in 1902. Pop (my father) was advised by his father, Fedor, to go to America as war would come again. Barney Hendler, a travel agent and hotel owner, made the arrangements, and on January 29, 1902, Pop was in America. On December 1, 1904 – Michal's wife, Feduňa, and their three children, Ned, Anna and Frank, arrived on Ellis Island. It is assumed that their names were originally recorded as Feduňa, Ned, Anna and Frank Senczyszyn and that their names were anglicized to Frances Sensheshin and Ned, Anna and Frank Sensheshin.

On June 6, 1940, Michal Senczyszyn's name was changed by Court Order to Michal Sensheshin. On August 25, 1943, Ned Sensheshin's name was changed by Court Order to Ned Senner. On the same date, August 25, 1943, Frank Sensheshin's name was changed by Court Order to Frank Senner.

In reference to my father (Pop), your great grandfather, I am enclosing a photostatic copy of a military pass issued to him in Europe in 1898 under his name at that time, Michal Senczyszyn.

I am also enclosing a photostatic copy of a Certificate of Naturalization that was issued to Pop on June 6, 1940, by the Common Pleas Court in Ebensburg, Pennsylvania, when he became a United States citizen. You will note that on the reverse side of this Certificate of Naturalization, that when he became a citizen, his name was changed by Order of the Court from Michal Sensczyszyn to Michal Sensheshin.

When your grandmother, Anna, my oldest sister was fifteen,
she met you grandfather who was staying at the boarding
house your great grandparents owned and operated. You
probably know from your mom he was a coal miner from
Poland who had stowed away on a ship to Baltimore when he
was nine to run away from the priests in Poland who always
kept beating him in the orphanage. He had a sister, too, who
went to Australia though we never heard much from them,
but your mom may know more. Your grandmother and
grandfather got married when she was fifteen and he was
twenty-seven. They had thirteen children and your mom was
the only girl. Most of your grandmother's sons, your uncles,
fought in World War II in both Europe and Asia. The younger
ones fought in Korea and Vietnam. I was a WASP (Women
Airforce Service Pilot) in World War II, the first women pilots
in the US Air Force, stationed first in British West Africa,
what is now Ghana, and then later in London during the Blitz.

Finally, I was stationed in Paris in the Air Transport
Command North Atlantic Wing at the Hotel Napoleon to
prepare De Gaulle's re-entry in France and his march into Paris.
We had to make it look like the French had liberated
themselves. My husband, your great uncle Harry, was
stationed in Biarritz.

I was so happy to send this to you, Jane. Let me know if
I can send you anything more.

Love,

Aunt Frances and Uncle Harry"

Jane read the letter over and over again and struggled with the
German on her great grandfather's military pass. The Ruthnian in
Cyrillic letters were a complete mystery to her, but she could understand some of the German from the German she had picked up and
from her Dutch. Every time she had expressed interest in learning
German, her Dutch in-laws and many other Dutch would immediately begin to discourage her as if the war had never ended. Now,
holding her own tangible history in her hands, she wished she had
listened to her own heart and mind.

Well, there was plenty of time left, she reminded herself.

She pondered on her great grandfather's fate for a long time after
that. He escaped World War I in Europe only to see his youngest

daughter and his grandsons fight for the us back in Europe and elsewhere.

Her great aunt would have said that this was in line with the family
tradition since Jane's great grandfather had been in the Austrian-
Hungarian army himself.

Jane had a different perspective on their family history. You can run
but you cannot hide.

When Jane was a child, her grandmother had given her her favorite
son's violin. This was the son who had been killed in World War ii.
Jane had been taking violin lessons at school and her grandmother
decided she should have her uncle George's violin and his music
books. Jane's grandfather had had the violin shipped from Europe for
his most cherished son. Jane remembered climbing up to the attic of
her grandmother's farmhouse with her sisters and grandmother to
look for the violin. Amongst the dust and cobwebs and ancient
editions of National Geographic, they found it in an oblong rectan-
gular violin case that resembled a triangle more than a rectangle. Scattered around the violin were music books, lessons for the violin, with
the handwritten name on them "George Witeof".

This was the handwriting of the young man in the portrait hanging
in the sitting room for guests who never came to visit. This was the
handwriting of the young man for whom the flag had been folded
triangularly which now rested underneath the portrait without a speck
of dusk. This was the handwriting of the young man whose sudden
death had plunged Jane's grandmother into depression for years and
whose death had left an indelible hole in Jane's mother's heart because
she had lost the only family member who thought it worth the while
to protect his little sister even though she was a girl. This was the handwriting Jane would always see when she opened her music lessons.

You can run but you cannot hide.

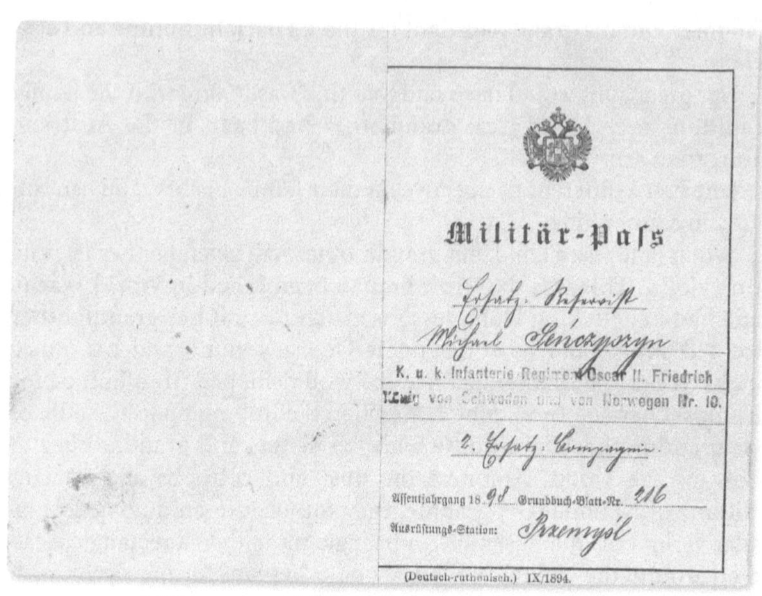

*Military pass, Michal Senczyszyn, issued 1898.*

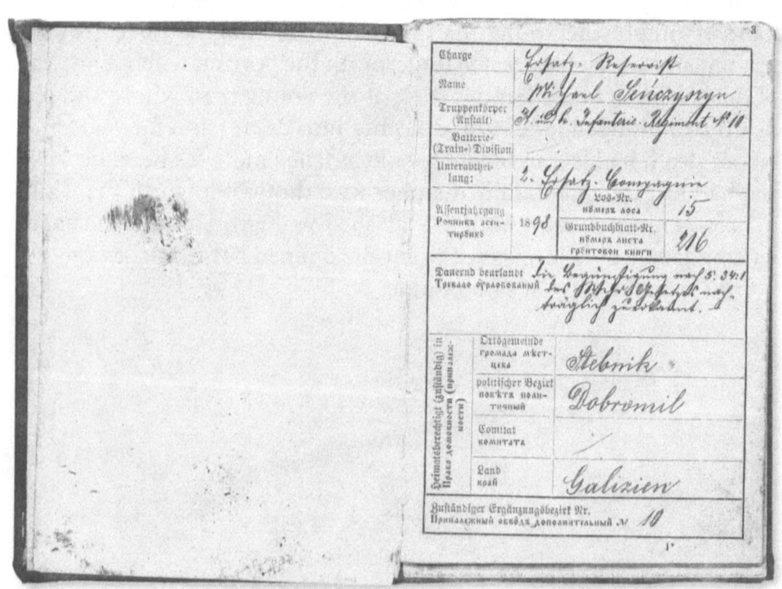

*Military pass, Michal Senszyszyn, p. 2–3.*

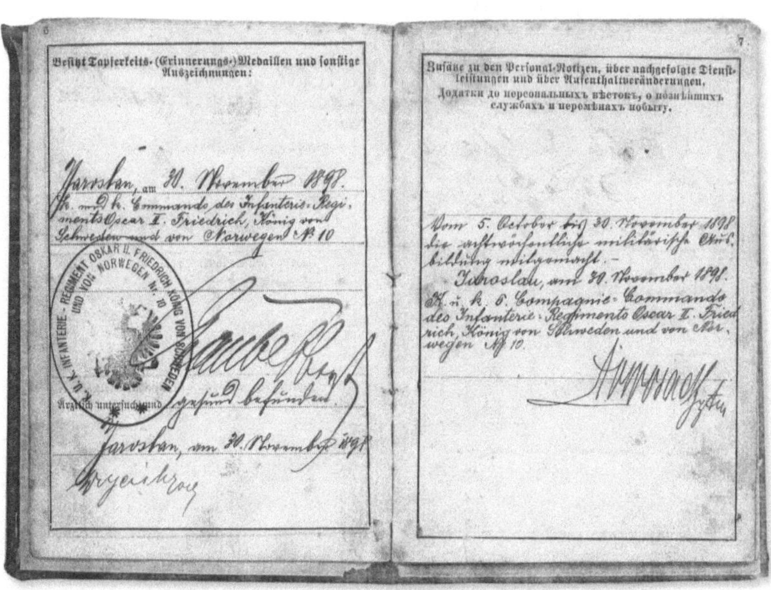

*Military pass, Michal Senczyszyn, p. 4–5.*

*Military pass, Michal Senczyszyn, p. 6–7.*

*Military pass, Michal Senczyszyn, p. 8–9.*

*Military pass, Michal Senczyszyn, p. 10–11.*

APLIKACYA DLA ZAGRANICZNEGO PRZEKAZU POCZTOWEGO.

Data.......................19......

Marka.......................

Suma.......................

Wypłacić (Payee).......................

Wieś.......................

Poczta.......................

Gmina.......................

Powiat.......................

Gubernia.......................

Wysyła (Sender).......................

Ulica.......................

Miasto.......................

Stan.......................

Numer.......................

---

Informacye

Po dalsze informacye co do naszych rozmaitych gałęzi działalności można się zwrócić do biura "American Railway Express" w każdym większym mieście Stanów Zjednoczonych, albo do każdego biura Towarzystwa "American Express Company", których adresa podajemy poniżej:

NEW YORK
65 Broadway (Head Office) 118 West 39th Street.
18 Chatham Square
BALTIMORE
19 East Baltimore St.
BOSTON
43 Franklin St.
BUFFALO
Main and Erie Sts.
CHICAGO
21 West Monroe St.
CINCINNATI
Fourth and Race Sts.
CLEVELAND
2048 East 9th St.
DETROIT
11 Fort St., West
KANSAS CITY
1125 McGee St.

LOS ANGELES
752 South Broadway
MILWAUKEE
368 Broadway
MINNEAPOLIS
619 Marquette Ave.
MONTREAL, CAN.
231 St. James St.
PHILADELPHIA
Wanamaker's (Main Floor—Centre)
PITTSBURGH
909 Liberty Ave.
ST. LOUIS
9th and Locust Sts.
SAN FRANCISCO
Market St. at Second
SEATTLE
804 Third Ave.
WASHINGTON
1328 F St., N. W.

Albo też napisz do naszego głównego biura:

"Foreign Money Order Department"

AMERICAN EXPRESS COMPANY

65 Broadway    New York

(A-1261. Polish)

---

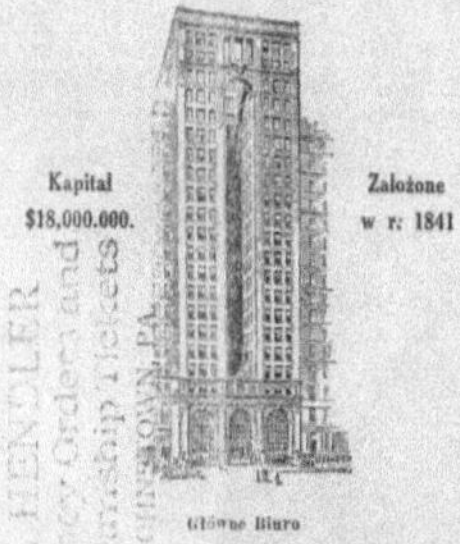

## Posyłanie Pieniędzy do Polski i do Galicyi



---

Jeżeli chcesz się poinformować co do najbezpieczniejszego, najtańszego i najlepszego sposobu posyłania pieniędzy do Polski i do Galicyi lub do jakiegokolwiek innego kraju poza granicami Stanów Zjednoczonych, lub też z jednego miasta do drugiego miasta tutaj w kraju, to przeczytaj następujące stronice niniejszej książeczki.

The American Express Company

zajmuje się specyalnie wysyłaniem pieniędzy, zarówno w kraju jakoteż i zagranicę. Posiada ono długoletnią reputacyę uczciwego prowadzenia interesów (Towarzystwo zostało założone w r. 1841), a wielki jego kapitał $18.000.000.00 i wielki zastęp doświadczonych urzędników, zapewniają bezwzględne bezpieczeństwo i doręczenie pieniędzy w jak najkrótszym czasie. Poniżej wymienione są rozmaite sposoby posyłania pieniędzy zagranicę.

Zagraniczne Przekazy Pieniężne

Najlepszy sposób wysyłania małych sum pieniężnych, lub do małych miasteczek lub wsi — to Zagraniczny Przekaz Pieniężny Towarzystwa American Express (Foreign Money Order). Gdy nadawca złoży u nas sumę którą chce wysłać, i poda imię, nazwisko i adres osoby, która ma je otrzymać, to my postaramy się o to by pieniądze osobie tej doręczono. Damy ci kwit na pieniądze, które u nas złożyłeś, a gdy adresata

nie można znaleść, to pieniądze będą ci zwrócone.

Na piątej stronicy niniejszej książeczki znajduje się formularz apikacyi dla nadania zagranicznego przekazu pieniężnego; celem otrzymania więcej formularzy tego rodzaju należy napisać do naszego biura "Foreign Money Order Department American Express Company, 65 Broadway, New York City."

Weksle Zagraniczne

Celem posyłania większych sum polecamy używania Weksli "American Express" (American Express Drafts) w Markach i Koronach, które są płatne w naszych biurach lub w głównych bankach w twoim kraju; weksel ten możesz sam wysłać do osoby, która pieniądze te ma otrzymać. Osoba ta może sama potem otrzymać wypłatę tego weksla prezentując go w banku na który był trasowany, albo też składając go w swoim banku miejscowym.

Sprzedajemy weksle po najniższej cenie, dołączając przy tem kwit do każdego weksla, tak że w razie utraty, można łatwo otrzymać duplikat lub też zwrot pieniędzy.

Pieniądze Wypłacone Telegraficznie

Jeżeli jednak chcesz, by pieniądze nadeszły do Polski prędzej niżby to było możliwe pocztą, to w takim razie wyślemy je w twoim imieniu drogą telegraficzną po cenach bardzo niskich. Banki w Polsce, z którymi korespondujemy, potwierdzają telegraficznie nasze zlecenia co do wypłaty pieniędzy, poczem my ciebie zawiadomimy, tak że natychmiast będziesz wiedział czy pieniądze nadeszły. Nic ci nie policzymy za zawiadomienie cię. Jakkolwiek nie możemy gwarantować doręczenia pieniędzy w ciągu jakiegokolwiek ściśle oznaczonego okresu czasu, ani też nie możemy być odpowiedzialni za zwłokę lub pomyłki towarzystw telegraficznych, to przecież ogólnie biorąc pieniądze posyłane telegraficznie, zazwyczaj są doręczane w ciągu kilku dni. Tak samo jak przy innych sposobach wysyłania pieniędzy, otrzymasz kwit za wysłaną sumę.

Depozyty w Bankach

Możemy złożyć pieniądze w twoim imieniu w jakimkolwiek banku lub kasie oszczędności w Polsce, albo też możemy otworzyć nowe konto w twoim imieniu w jakimkolwiek z tych banków. Zwracamy ci twoją książkę bankową albo ci posyłamy na jakikolwiek adres nie policzając za to kosztów dodatkowych. Posyłając nam pieniądze w tym celu należy podać nazwę i adres banku jakoteż imię, nazwisko i adres depozytora w sposób następujący: "Pocztowa Kasa Oszczędności, Warszawa," for account of (na rachunek) John Jones, Smithville, Ohio, U. S. A." i należy też dołączyć trzy wzorki własnoręcznego podpisu (jeżeli rozchodzi się o nowe konto bankowe) albo książeczkę bankową (jeżeli zaś Konto Bankowe otworzone było).

*Immigration folder for Polish-speaking immigrants.*

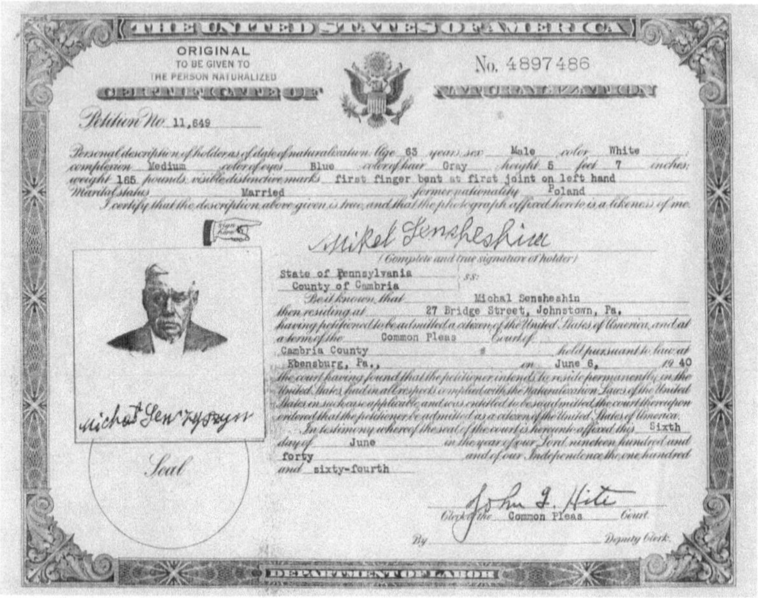

THE UNITED STATES OF AMERICA

ORIGINAL
TO BE GIVEN TO
THE PERSON NATURALIZED

No. 4897486

CERTIFICATE OF NATURALIZATION

Petition No. 11,649

Personal description of holder as of date of naturalization: Age 63 years; sex Male color White complexion Medium color of eyes Blue color of hair Gray height 5 feet 7 inches; weight 165 pounds; visible distinctive marks first finger bent at first joint on left hand
Marital status Married former nationality Poland
I certify that the description above given is true, and that the photograph affixed hereto is a likeness of me.

Mikel Sensheshin
(Complete and true signature of holder)

Michał Senczyszyn

Seal

State of Pennsylvania
County of Cambria ss:
Be it known, that Michal Sensheshin
then residing at 27 Bridge Street, Johnstown, Pa.
having petitioned to be admitted a citizen of the United States of America, and at a term of the Common Pleas Court of Cambria County held pursuant to law at Ebensburg, Pa., on June 6, 1940
the court having found that the petitioner intends to reside permanently in the United States, had in all respects complied with the Naturalization Laws of the United States in such case applicable, and was entitled to be so admitted, the court thereupon ordered that the petitioner be admitted as a citizen of the United States of America.
In testimony whereof the seal of the court is hereunto affixed this Sixth day of June in the year of our Lord nineteen hundred and forty and of our Independence the one hundred and sixty-fourth

John F. Hite
Clerk of the Common Pleas Court.
By Deputy Clerk.

DEPARTMENT OF LABOR

*Michal Senczyszyn's Certificate of Naturalization.*

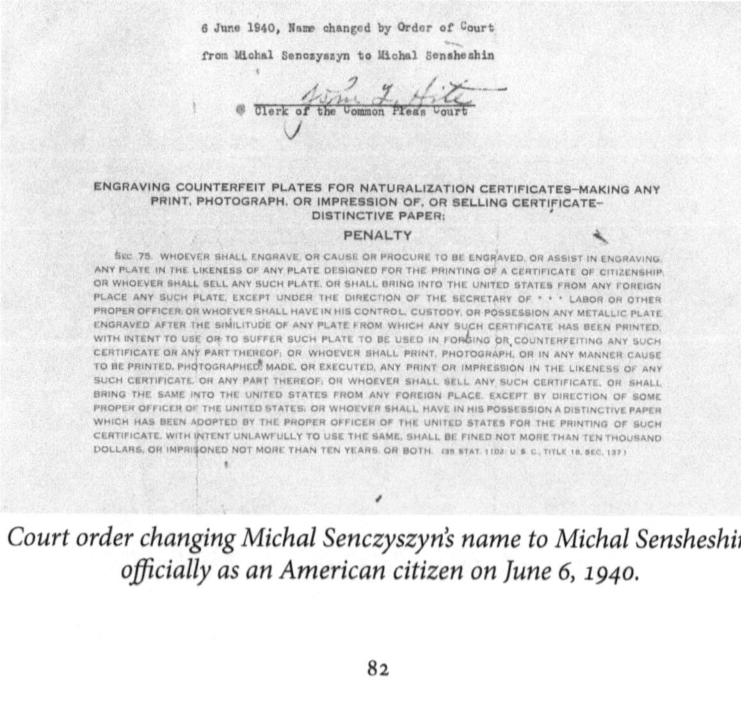

6 June 1940, Name changed by Order of Court
from Michal Senczyszyn to Michal Sensheshin

John F. Hite
Clerk of the Common Pleas Court

ENGRAVING COUNTERFEIT PLATES FOR NATURALIZATION CERTIFICATES–MAKING ANY PRINT, PHOTOGRAPH, OR IMPRESSION OF, OR SELLING CERTIFICATE–DISTINCTIVE PAPER;

PENALTY

SEC. 75. WHOEVER SHALL ENGRAVE, OR CAUSE OR PROCURE TO BE ENGRAVED, OR ASSIST IN ENGRAVING, ANY PLATE IN THE LIKENESS OF ANY PLATE DESIGNED FOR THE PRINTING OF A CERTIFICATE OF CITIZENSHIP, OR WHOEVER SHALL SELL ANY SUCH PLATE, OR SHALL BRING INTO THE UNITED STATES FROM ANY FOREIGN PLACE ANY SUCH PLATE, EXCEPT UNDER THE DIRECTION OF THE SECRETARY OF * * * LABOR OR OTHER PROPER OFFICER; OR WHOEVER SHALL HAVE IN HIS CONTROL, CUSTODY, OR POSSESSION ANY METALLIC PLATE ENGRAVED AFTER THE SIMILITUDE OF ANY PLATE FROM WHICH ANY SUCH CERTIFICATE HAS BEEN PRINTED, WITH INTENT TO USE OR TO SUFFER SUCH PLATE TO BE USED IN FORGING OR COUNTERFEITING ANY SUCH CERTIFICATE OR ANY PART THEREOF; OR WHOEVER SHALL PRINT, PHOTOGRAPH, OR IN ANY MANNER CAUSE TO BE PRINTED, PHOTOGRAPHED, MADE, OR EXECUTED, ANY PRINT OR IMPRESSION IN THE LIKENESS OF ANY SUCH CERTIFICATE, OR ANY PART THEREOF; OR WHOEVER SHALL SELL ANY SUCH CERTIFICATE, OR SHALL BRING THE SAME INTO THE UNITED STATES FROM ANY FOREIGN PLACE, EXCEPT BY DIRECTION OF SOME PROPER OFFICER OF THE UNITED STATES; OR WHOEVER SHALL HAVE IN HIS POSSESSION A DISTINCTIVE PAPER WHICH HAS BEEN ADOPTED BY THE PROPER OFFICER OF THE UNITED STATES FOR THE PRINTING OF SUCH CERTIFICATE, WITH INTENT UNLAWFULLY TO USE THE SAME, SHALL BE FINED NOT MORE THAN TEN THOUSAND DOLLARS, OR IMPRISONED NOT MORE THAN TEN YEARS, OR BOTH. (35 STAT. 1102; U. S. C., TITLE 18, SEC. 137.)

*Court order changing Michal Senczyszyn's name to Michal Sensheshin officially as an American citizen on June 6, 1940.*

*One of George Witeof's music books.*

"Jane, I'm so glad you've decided to register here in Louvain and continue to pursue your PhD here with me. You've got a great topic!" exclaimed Professor Stanford. His new office in Louvain, not much bigger than a cubbyhole, could hardly contain his boisterous spirit at seeing Jane again.

"I'll make sure she keeps working at it," her husband interjected reminding her PhD advisor that he was in the picture, too.

"Yes, that's what every PhD candidate needs, support from the home!" Professor Stanford embellished.

"Papa, are you really going to help mama?" the ever-astute Lisa asked while Danielle climbed all over her mother's lap. Just the hint of mother and wife redirecting her attention elsewhere brought on a mobilization in both husband and children not unlike that just before a war.

"Well, we had better get going. The kids are getting impatient," her husband stood up to leave and shook Professor Stanford's hand in the normal Dutch, but curt, fashion. The children tumbled after him.

Professor Stanford stayed behind his door with his hand on the doorknob while he held it ajar to get word with Jane on his own.

"I admire your strength to continue. Courage!" He clenched his fist and bent his arm up as a sign of strength. "Courage!" he exclaimed again.

Jane let the tutors and professors who supported her know she had officially registered in Louvain and shared her email address with them. Everyone welcomed her back. She had a special message for Dr. Lebenstein because she had heard down the grapevine that after years of waiting, and because at the last minute all the foreign candidates they had had pulled out, Dr. Lebenstein was awarded Professor Stanford's professorship.

"Dear Professor Lebenstein,
First and foremost, I would like to congratulate you on your professorship. I would also like to inform you that I am now officially registered in Louvain to continue my PhD and would like to give you my Louvain email address. I would also like to ask whether I could quote from you latest book which, as you know, includes some research that supports my own.

Congratulations on the Ezra Pound Society award, too! I happened to be in Rapallo the year before, but just for vacation. Isn't it beautiful?

Of course, I'd like to invite you to my viva when I defend, and if I may, could I be so bold as to ask you to invite me to your inaugural address?

Thanks in advance.
Kind regards,
Jane
PS. I promise you if you invite me to your inaugural address, I will only sit in the corner and smile and keep my mouth shut…
'Hell hath no fury like the tongue of a woman.' The Bard"

Dr. Lebenstein's response was overwhelming.

"Dear Jane,
Glad to hear you have not given up. Even when I am a professor officially, just keep calling me John. Of course, you may quote me and I would love to give you a copy, but my

publisher would be dismayed, so check it out from the library
to save yourself a buck.

Yes, I do expect an invitation to your public defense at the very
least and since you must defend twice in Belgium, you'd better
include me in on the private defense, too. My inaugural
address will take place most likely in January 2008 because
everything is so well organized here in Leiden and years ahead
of time, too.

Jane without a tongue is like a cauliflower without salt.
John"

It had been years since Jane had received a compliment like that from
a man. It was as if she had forgotten that compliments like that existed
and could even be remotely intended for her ears. Professor Lebenstein complimented her intelligence, too, and that compliment was
more important to her than any other.

About a week later, Jane made a fantastic lunch for her whole
family so that they could eat al fresco and enjoy one of the last days of
summer. Her husband promptly complained about the food and about
how he didn't want to have to sit down in the middle of the day. Jane
reminded him that she had made his and the children's favorite dishes
and the children would enjoy the time with him since he was back at
work after their long vacation in France. He continued complaining
over and over again and since her pleas were futile, she just stopped
listening and tried to make the best of it for the children.

When he realized she had tuned him out, he screamed, "You don't
listen to me! Why don't you listen to me?"

Jane replied calm and curtly, "At least Professor Lebenstein listens
to me."

With that, her husband stood up, and without any regard for the
children, tipped the table over with all the hot food on it. The children
saw it coming just in time and managed to slip out of their seats and
run just before the hot food started sliding down to the ground on
their side of the table.

The day started out bright and sunny. Jane went for a run in the morning and was getting the kids ready for school and daycare. Lisa was now in school and Danielle would start next year. Jane looked forward to the freedom that would bring especially with regard to her research.

Lately, since Jane had registered at the university in Louvain, her husband had started trying to persuade her to have another child. Jane was stunned by the suggestion. She had always wanted more than two children and he had always stood his ground that he only wanted two. Now that she knew the realities of raising children, and even though she was married, in the end she did most of the raising and felt like she was on her own. Getting him to be more involved with the children and running the household was more exhausting than chasing after the kids. It was just easier to do it herself.

It's easy to want to have another child if you don't do any of the work yourself, Jane had thought to herself a number of times. Besides, she had other dreams for her life that she wanted to pursue.

For some reason, this morning her husband didn't leave for work on time. The routine she had established with the girls to get them moving in the morning had been thrown completely ajar. Then he stood right in front of her as she was walking into the kitchen. Her daughters looked on while they ate breakfast. He wouldn't let her pass. If she moved from side to side in order to try and pass him, he blocked her like it was some kind of sports game.

"I need to get in the kitchen to make their lunches. Would you like to help me?" He backed off. Jane figured the rhetorical question would ruin his standing.

Then while she was rushing the children up to the bathroom to brush their teeth, her husband did it again. He stood in front of the bathroom door and blocked her entrance with the children behind her.

"Please, the children are going to be late and they'll blame the parents." He stood motionless. She tried to pass from either side, but just as in the kitchen, he blocked her every attempt to get in.

"Why are you doing this? The children need to brush their teeth and get to school!" He finally let up and let the kids and Jane brush their teeth.

Then as they were about to leave, he stood in front of the front door. Again he wouldn't let Jane and the children pass and the door behind him was closed. "Please, why are you doing this? Don't you need to go to work? The children are going to be late!"

And with that last word came the swooshing sound she would never forget; the sound of the first punch. It knocked the wind out of her as his fist landed squarely on her breast. She caught her breast and bent over as the pain radiated like a million lightning bolts from the point of impact to the outskirts of her breast. Unable to hold her keys and purse in the intense pain, they dropped to the floor.

For all her exercising, and for all his laziness, in that split second she realized men were always physically stronger than women. It was an innate part of the male muscle mass that was prone to misuse in order to dominate. A powerless feeling of defenselessness and vulnerability swept over her while she tried to remain standing in front of her daughters. Her spirit sunk, at least for a second.

Remembering her children made her forget her pain and she raised up and faced him. "Get out of the way!" He pushed her back in to the hallway and she landed with her left shoulder against the wall. Another point of impact radiated lightning bolts of pain in a circle around it. This was different from the first blow, though, where the pain was so intense because the impact had been squarely on soft tissue.

After she hit the wall, he ran back in to the kitchen. Jane grabbed her purse and keys which had fallen to ground, quickly opened the door, grabbed the children's hands and ran to the car.

She dropped them off at school and daycare, full of profusive apologies, that it had been such a crazy morning, but now they're finally here, and proceeded directly to the police.

At the police station, Jane was treated sympathetically and gingerly by the young officer who took her statement and the female officer who took pictures of her bruises.

Just as she had signed the statement, the sergeant walked in.

"You do realize your marriage is over."

Jane listened to him stunned.

"We're about to go and arrest him at his employer. It's the end of your marriage."

"Why are you telling me this?"

"Because women like you don't get abused."

"I beg your pardon."

"Women like you don't get abused. You know. Smart women."

"Are you suggesting I inflicted these injuries upon myself?"

The sergeant jumped a little. "No, not necessarily."

Jane sat in silence and looked at the sergeant head on. Her first encounter with the justice system was instantaneously a baptism of fire. Despite the fact that she was clearly the victim and she did what the authorities always told you to do, go immediately to the authorities if you have been abused, she did not have the benefit of the doubt because she was a woman. The fact that she was a smart woman impaired her position as a victim even more. The sergeant clearly assumed there was an element of conniving in her complaint. Jane felt overcome by a feeling that though she had assumed the authorities were on her side, the odds were stacked against her. Nothing had changed since her mother had told her repeatedly when she was young, "But if I divorce him, who would believe me?" In an instant, the sergeant revealed to her that what she forever considered her mother's excuse was in reality the cold, hard truth.

There was also another part of Jane that was not ready to admit that her marriage was over. There in the police station alone, she sat surrounded by officers and just freshly beaten by the one person in the world she had always trusted the most. She was clearly not ready for battle.

"Could you just call him and give him a warning? I don't know whether I'm ready to initiate divorce proceedings. I think that will give him enough warning not to do this again."

The officers looked at each other disappointedly. What they did not tell Jane was that when a domestic violence incident was reported immediately, there was no hearsay involved and it was an instant conviction. This conviction would have revved up their statistics for the month which guaranteed their monthly bonus. That was also the reason why so many officers were standing in the room. All of them could claim they were involved in the complaint and could therefore claim their bonus. The inalienable rights of safety and privacy did not apply to beaten women when they clearly needed it most. Financial gain, and in this as in most cases, male financial gain since there was only one female officer in the room, superseded Jane's seemingly inalienable rights. The rights of women, children and all minorities end where white, male patriarchal privilege begins. That privilege begins with overriding benefit of the doubt for white men, especially educated, white men which makes the burden of proof virtually insurmountable for anyone who speaks up against them and does not fit the same bill.

"Yeah, we can just call him," the sergeant replied.

The police had called Jane's husband at work and in the days that followed, she realized she had made a grave miscalculation. The police were right in their estimation of his reaction. He didn't take it as a warning but as an act of war. Her marriage was over and he was bent on revenge. The next week, he worked at home and every morning when she woke, he was standing over her on her side of the bed. He would not leave her out of his sight. The children were extremely on edge.

Jane knew she had to get away but she didn't know how to with the children. Since he had started working at home, he picked up the children and took them to all their lessons. Everything that had to do with the children that he previously had been more than happy to leave to her so he could come and go as he pleased, he had now completely taken over. He knew she was at the point of leaving him, but would do everything to prevent that, even use the children for that purpose.

When he took the children to school, she called the shelter hotline.

"Hi, this is the Domestic Violence Hotline, how can I help you?"

"Hi, I really need your help. My husband beat me about a week ago and I reported it to the police. The atmosphere is explosive at home now and I'm really afraid for my children. I'm an American citizen here and I don't have any family to go to."

"Don't you have friends you can go to?"

"They all have families themselves. If I do, I don't think I could stay for long enough. I really need a shelter."

"But you do have a network?"

"I have friends, but I don't have any family here."

"What's your education level?"

"What?"

"Your education level. Where is the last place you attended school?"

"The University of Leiden."

"Oh, well, you don't need us then. You've got plenty of contacts."

"I'm a foreign woman here alone with my children. I'm about to get his entire family against me when he tells them I reported it to the police. I don't have any income right now. I'm unemployed so I can't pay for accommodation myself."

"Yeah, but you can figure out something. You're highly educated."

"Yeah, but a piece of paper is not going to protect me and my children from my husband. Can't you give me the address of the nearest shelter? He'll be home any second and I don't want him to catch me on the phone with you."

"I'm sorry I can't give the address of a shelter because I think you don't need it. Shelters are terrible for children. See whether you can stay with friends."

"No, I want the name of a shelter. If he starts harassing my friends because they helped me, I won't have anyone left. And besides, every morning when I wake up, he's standing over me. It's really creepy."

"I'm sorry. Like I said, I don't think you need it."

"I thought I was safe in the Netherlands with my children because you have shelters for abused women and their children."

"The Netherlands is a very hypocritical country. Good luck to you. Goodbye."

And with that, Jane heard the Domestic Violence Hotline hanging up the phone and the click of the front door opening. Her husband was home.

Jane made a harrowing decision. She knew her husband wanted to kill her and she feared that if the atmosphere in the home got any more threatening, Lisa and Danielle could be victims, too. Jane thought if she could remove herself from this lethal equation, the atmosphere in their home might simmer down for her daughters and she could return for them. If she was dead, there would be no more option of return and her death in the face of a violent father would cause irreparable, if not irreversible, damage to her daughters. Jane could hear their voices in her mind's eye, "Mama, where are you? Mama, why weren't you there to protect us?" Jane knew that even if she were in heaven, hearing her children's voices searching for and pleading for her would instantly render even God's paradise into an eternal, harrowing hell.

"Paradise is at the feet of the mothers. That is what Mohammed taught us," a fellow student of Turkish descent had told her at university. Her conscience echoed, "And for this reason, Jane, for Lisa and Danielle, you cannot die."

Jane had read that when you escape an abuser, you must have a secret bag packed and ready with clothes, cash, credit cards and travel documents. Jane didn't have that option. Her husband was home constantly watching her like a hawk. Whenever he ran errands, he took the family car. If she withdrew any money from their joint banking account, the only bank account she had, he could see it on the internet immediately. The only way she could access money was if she withdrew money from their joint credit card. He wouldn't see those withdrawals for another few weeks when the statement came. That would give her access to funds and buy her time.

"Oh, God, Lisa and Danielle," she thought. "What if I miscalculate him again and he does something to them after I leave?" But in her heart she knew he would only expect her to leave with the children, never on her own. He knew his control of her had caused her love for him to evaporate and in his desperation to control her now, he would use any means necessary and the only means he had left were the children.

She had not stopped running or working out, so she asked him whether she could take the car after dinner to go work out at the gym.

She said riding her bike through the park didn't seem like the safest option now that the days were shorter and it was dark so early.

"Yeah, no problem," he said. "What time will you be back?"

"The gym closes at 10:00, so I'll be back before then."

She took her purse and walked out the door. It still contained the children's American passports from their vacation in France with his parents. Her heart sank as she closed the door behind her. She stopped for a moment but quickly regained herself since the shifting light from the kitchen window meant he was peering out at her and had just raised the curtain a fraction of an inch to monitor her every step. She knew if she divulged any emotion her plan would be foiled.

She walked to the car, opened the door and started the car as if it was the most normal thing in the world. Once she was out of the street, she drove directly to the automated cash machine and withdrew the maximum daily allowance from their credit card.

From there Jane drove to her exchange-year parents' house in the north of the country. When she arrived and told the story and expected support, she got the complete opposite reaction from her exchange-year mother.

"What did you do to deserve being beaten?"

Stunned for a second by her exchange mother's reaction, she rose to leave.

"Where do you think you're going?"

"Well, I'm not staying here that's for sure." Jane swung the door open, walked diagonally over the lawn and towards her car. Her exchange-year parents stood in the door.

Her exchange mother kept screaming, "Where do you think you're going?"

Jane opened her car door, sat down, started the ignition and drove to her exchange brother's house. He and his wife opened the door; luckily, they had heard her knocking at such a late hour. She didn't want to use the doorbell because their infant was sleeping.

Her exchange brother's wife was flabbergasted, "Oh my God, Jane, he beat you?"

"I couldn't get a place in a shelter for me and the children. Since I reported it to the police, he's been working at home and won't let me take the children anywhere. I had to leave them behind."

"Oh God, Jane. Come in."

Jane had found the refuge and support she needed, if only temporarily. Her exchange brother told her the next morning that, of course, she could stay for the time being, but she needed to look for another solution. She called all the places she could think of where she might get help. They all referred her back to the domestic violence shelters where she had already been refused.

She thought of one place, the Catholic University of Louvain where she had just registered. Now that she was a student, she had access to temporary accommodation which was also affordable. She called the university and they offered her a temporary room at an abbey just outside Louvain with breakfast and dinner included. She booked it and told them she would be arriving the next morning.

"Oh yes, do they have family accommodation, too, in case I want to bring my children?"

"Yes, they do and it's available now. Would you like me to contact the abbey to say that you'll need the family accommodation?"

"No, not right now, but thank you. I need to work it out with their school first. For now, I'll just take the room, but maybe I'll bring the children down during their midterm break next week."

"Let us know in advance, please."

"By all means," Jane answered politely and excitedly at the prospect of a solution.

After Jane hung up the phone with the student accommodation authority in Louvain, something began to nag her. If she did go to Belgium, she would be crossing an international border with the children, wouldn't that be considered international child abduction now that she most likely was going to be in divorce proceedings soon? She recalled vaguely having seen something on television once that discussed cases like this.

Jane called another family she had lived with. The lady's brother just happened to be a rather famous retired family law judge. Jane called the judge and he confirmed what she feared. Indeed, if she took the children across the border on her own during divorce proceedings, it would not be considered international child abduction as long as you had written permission for taking the children.

"However, be very careful, Jane. Many fathers give permission and then they claim the mother forged the note. The father usually gets the benefit of the doubt because taking the children across an international border during divorce proceedings does not look good. The fact that you couldn't a get place in a shelter for you and the children won't hold water with a Dutch judge. A judicial authority will never admit the system doesn't work. And Jane, one more thing."

"Yes?"

"Keep all the police reports about abuse. Whoever leaves the house during divorce proceedings forfeits their right to it after the divorce for whatever reason, even abuse. You might get the benefit of the doubt if you can show you had to flee but it depends on the judge. In any case, the judge will rule that the children should remain in the parental home, so if you lose the house, you may very well lose the children, too. You must prevent that, Jane. I've seen too many cases where once the mother is out of the picture, the father starts abusing the children. In the male mind, women and children are still property, Jane, and the law does not take into account independent women who have the courage to leave and protect their children.

"It's ok to take a breather now and let the situation simmer down. But you must go back after ten days and don't start the divorce proceedings until then. Take care, Jane. You have a very long and rough road ahead of you."

Jane put down the phone silently as she heard the click on the other end of the line. She borrowed clothes from her exchange brothers' wife because she had none of her own to take with her. That evening, Jane called her children to tell them she was going away for awhile, but she would be back very soon.

"Mama, when are you coming home?" asked Lisa, who was five.

"Soon, honey. Very soon."

Danielle, now three, mumbled something before she hung up.

Jane was glad she would be wearing another woman's clothes in Belgium. It was the perfect disguise to hide her shame for leaving her children. The pain of shame and disgrace is piercing.

Jane called her children every evening from the abbey and would cry herself to sleep every night. One morning one of the nuns in the abbey approached her in the hallway on the way to breakfast and asked, "Why do you cry at night, child?"

"I miss my children so much."

"Do you have a picture to show me?"

Jane pulled out her wallet pictures of her children and showed them to the nun.

"You are blessed with such beautiful children! Remember, all the work you do here is really for them. That is the nature of the mother. When you have achieved all you have for them and they have a better life, the pain that is so poignant now will be forgotten."

Jane's eyes welled up. The nun grabbed her to give her a hug.

"Now, now. Come on, you've got a lot of work to do today. You can't concentrate if you let yourself cry in the morning. Save your tears for in the evening when they will be tears of joy for all that you have accomplished today for your children."

It was moments like these in her life abroad that Jane realized how hard it was having her own mother so far away. Luckily, during her journey through life and overseas she would occasionally run into someone who, for just for a moment and at the right moment, would take her under her wing like a surrogate mother.

Jane met with her advisor to discuss what she had already finished a few years ago and what she still needed to do. Jane also was considering whether to tell her advisor she was about to file for divorce, but first wanted to see how the meeting would go. She could always tell him later if she had to and she didn't want to dampen his enthusiasm for her research since she had picked up her PhD again.

She decided to start the meeting on a lighter note since she knew Professor Stanford loved trivia. "Did I ever tell you that my dad was delivered by William Carlos Williams? He was my grandparents' and my dad's family doctor." The response she got was not the one she had anticipated.

Professor Stanford was silent and he looked at her with a serious stare. Jane had never experienced Professor Stanford so intense before. After a minute, he said, "Sit down, Jane."

"Sure, ok."

"Jane, you need to look into your DNA."

"What?"

"I know you've concentrated on Eliot and Pound for your research, but you need to look into your DNA."

"Why?"

"Jane, Williams had numerous affairs."

"Are you suggesting…"

"Jane, talk to your dad and look into your DNA. You need to know all you can before you can defend your dissertation and for the sake of your research. Williams was highly critical of Eliot the way you are. He told Eliot to name his sources as early as 'Prufrock' and named them for him just in case. As you know from your research, Pound was doing the same thing later after *The Waste Land*. Williams distrusted Eliot from the beginning just like you have since you were a student. Jane, you have to look into your DNA."

After the meeting, which, believe it or not, took somewhat of a natural course after its bombshell opening, Jane went back to the library and looked up pictures of William Carlos Williams. She had not even been able to tell Professor Stanford about her impending divorce. As the pictures came up, Jane was astounded to see that Williams and her father were the spitting image of each other as young and middle-aged men.

The floor beneath her feet suddenly got lighter. Pending between her future and her past, both of which now were completely unknown to her, Jane decided to put the past in a box for now and concentrate on the future and her children. The past would always be there for her to look into, the future was yet to be determined.

Besides, she couldn't handle looking into her DNA right now with life as she knew it falling apart. She knew the most important thing was keeping her children from having that same feeling as much as she could. Jane went back to the abbey in search of some peace.

O Lord Thou pluckest me out

O Lord Thou pluckest

Gentile or Jew

Jane was packing to go home again. She didn't want to be burdened with anything new, nor did she want to lose focus of what was most pressing right now: her and her children's future. She also didn't want to speak to anyone about what had transpired the Friday before in Professor Stanford's office. She feared it would raise eyebrows about her mental health. She knew from her own parents' failed marriage that it was the card her father always wanted to use to disparage her mother's stories of abuse. Since Jane had been to the police, she knew little had changed since her mother's time. It was not a good time at all to bring up William Carlos Williams and a possible affair, if not worse, with her grandmother.

Jane did one thing just in case the atmosphere was still untenable at the house. She didn't check out of the abbey.

When Jane got home that evening, her mother-in-law was at the house. Jane was not surprised his family decided they needed to help with the children. Funny they never wanted to help her so that she could progress in her career and outside the home.

"Jane, what do you think you're doing to your family?"

"Have you asked your son what he's doing to his family? He's responsible for his behavior and needs to keep his hands to himself."

"But that's no reason to end a marriage! What did you do to deserve it?"

"I'll be the judge of that. I underestimated you. I thought your views on women's rights were rather progressive, but it seems that is just window dressing. When your son is accused of domestic violence, you blame the victim to protect your own name, or perhaps to hide some ugly secrets of your own. Do me and my daughters a favor. Go back to your 1950s time warp and make tea for your husband."

Her mother-in-law froze in indignation. Jane knew she had won. Her mother-in-law left and slammed the front door behind her. By this time, Jane's daughters had witnessed everything from the stairs. Jane looked up to them.

She smiled at them proudly, beaming happily at the sight of them again. "You can come down now." Jane knew they only had an hour before her husband would be home.

Jane's husband was now home.

"So I heard you were rude to my mother."

"I'm not surprised that's her side of the story."

"Are you coming back?"

"Are you going to get help?" Jane knew this was a rhetorical question. They had gotten help before and miraculously, during the few sessions they had had with a therapist, he would talk. This was completely against his nature at home where a simple question about buying a new lamp could go unanswered for years. As a result, Jane had started making decisions on her own and would just weather his imminent criticism in the aftermath. And so began her alienation from him which was completed when his physical abuse started. Now she understood why the help they sought was never successful. He would take on the guise of a sensitive, friendly man in the presence of another, especially a therapist, thereby portraying her as the ambitious, demanding wife. Her first boss had once warned her, "Be careful. I respect your ambition and drive, but there are many people who consider ambitious women to be aggressive. I've seen it before. It's amazing. Depending on your gender, the terms are precisely interchanged either positively or negatively. A man with an ambitious aggression is something to admire. A woman who is ambitious is aggressive and must be quashed."

Jane's husband finally answered her, "No. Why should I get help? You're the one who needs help. Going to the police and saying I beat you."

"So those bruises just happened on their own?"

He was silent. "Get out."

"I'm not going anywhere."

He walked out of the room and stormed upstairs. Jane quickly went through the mail on the living room desk to see if anything had arrived for her. In one of the desk trays, she saw the envelope from Yale with the copies of Eliot's letters to Pound and Pound's letters to John Quinn, the New York attorney and manuscript collector in whose attic the manuscripts for *The Waste Land* had been found with Pound's edits which had previously been unknown. Underneath the envelope were Jane's handwritten notes for her dissertation. She grabbed them and hid them underneath her pile of mail while she heard her husband stomp down the stairs again.

The sight of the envelope and her notes had given her an epiphany moment into a previously unresolved mystery in her husband's family history. Just before his mother was about to turn in her master's thesis, all her notes and her manuscript disappeared never to be found again. Before the age of computers and copiers, often the first draft was the only draft. Mortally discouraged, his mother had never attempted to recover any of it or had even tried to work out something with her advisor so that she could get her degree.

In a flash, Jane had solved the mystery. His father, her father-in-law, had destroyed her work in an effort to control her. Jane knew she could not let that happen to her.

"Are you stealing my mail?"

"Of course not, you're not the only person who receives mail in this house. I have a right to privacy. I see you've taken the liberty of opening some of my mail. Thank you for respecting my privacy."

"It's my mail, too."

"No, it's not. It's addressed to me. How many times have you done this before?"

"Get out!"

"I'm not going anywhere!"

He thrust his face into hers and spat as he spoke, "Get out! Run to Lebenstein and his blue eyes! That's where the children got their blues eyes, isn't it?" He pushed her out of the living room and into the hallway. She landed on her shoulder as she crashed to the floor, clutching her mail and the manuscripts to her. They scattered all over the floor as she tried to break the impact when she fell. She scrambled to pick them up again as he approached her, towering above her. Struggling to get up quickly, she feared the kick of his boot.

She managed to open the heavy, Dutch front door and just made it halfway through the opening. He grabbed her arm and held her as he slammed the door on her breast. Just like the first time, the pain from the point of impact radiated like lightning bolts through the soft tissue. The blow had been twofold this time since the edge of the door opening had also jolted her back. She gasped at the pain but kept moving because this time she was not caught by surprise like the first time his rage had exploded into violence.

Still clutching her work, Jane ran to the car and just managed to yell back at him. "Both their grandmothers have blue eyes! Is this what this is about, you're insanely jealous? Oh God, it's worse than I thought."

"I'm so sorry, Jane! I'll get help! I promise!" He stood in the doorway which had just been his weapon, pleading. "Are you going to get a divorce?"

"Of course I am!" she yelled back and caught a glimpse of her daughters standing in an upstairs window watching her leave again.

"Oh God have mercy," she prayed as she started her car and drove back to the abbey in Louvain.

Back in the abbey, Jane had to find ways to get through the day and the night. She had a conference coming up, and another professor at Louvain had advised her she should be there. It was going to be held in Utrecht, back in the Netherlands, in a few weeks time and a famous Modernist scholar from America was going to be there. Jane hoped she would be home then close to her children, but also not miss an opportunity that might help them build a future since she soon would be on her own with two small daughters.

Jane pulled the manuscripts from their envelope from Yale. She read the first one in the pile from 1915.

> "My dear Pound,
> I am very glad to hear from you, and it is certainly very kind of you to make these efforts on my behalf. I enclose a copy of the Lady…."

How very different from the threats of the later letters. Jane checked the later letters and their dates. Handwritten, on an otherwise typed two-page letter with Faber and Faber letterhead at the end of a letter from 1933, was Eliot's threat to Pound:

"Solicitors <u>ARE</u> expensive."

Why, Jane thought, would Eliot be threatening his former mentor with lawyers? She knew Pound was poor and more or less penniless in Italy by then, and if you are poor, lawyers are an impossibility. But why would Eliot entrust his poetry to Pound and then, almost twenty years later, threaten a penniless poet with lawyers? She went back to the letter from 1915, and then checked the published version of the same letter. She looked back at the copy of the original.

The text of the letter mentioned another short poem that had been enclosed along with "Portrait of the Lady", but the poem was not included with the original letter. There was a poem, "Suppressed Complex", included at the end of the published version of the letter. A footnote mentioned it had come from another collection at another library, the Berg Collection at the New York Public Library. Jane chuckled for a minute because Mrs. Eliot was so restrictive in giving scholars permission to see the real manuscripts, which made it very hard indeed to confirm whether anything that had been published mirrored the original exactly. The published letters and manuscripts were always, since Eliot's death, the product of Mrs. Eliot's editing. One was left to assume Mrs. Eliot's presentation of the published "facts" was correct without being able to validate their accuracy. Funny that academics did not subject Mrs. Eliot to the same rigor they demanded of each other and especially their students, Jane thought.

"How can we know for sure this is the poem Eliot included?" she thought aloud to herself. Other than the mention of "Portrait of a Lady", nothing in the rest of the letter alluded to anything that might indicate that "Suppressed Complex" was indeed the poem Eliot had sent Pound along with "Portrait of a Lady". How did a poem that had previously been in Pound's collection of Eliot's letters suddenly end up in New York? Jane mused.

The word "suppressed" intrigued her for a minute. She had seen that word somewhere in the letters before. Somewhere in the letters that had not yet been published since Eliot's letters, at that time, had only been published up until 1922. For years, scholars and the public alike pleaded with Mrs. Eliot to publish his letters beyond 1922. For years, she remained staunchly silent on the subject, dumbfounding those who had assisted her with the first volume of letters. They had had the later letters in their hands and one person even remembered those letters in a box on the backseat of a car ready to be edited.

But then suddenly, the letters disappeared again back into university and public libraries and personal vaults scattered around the entire world, virtually irretrievable for scholars and the general public at large. Those scholars who could afford to view the original manuscripts and letters and had received permission from Mrs. Eliot to do so had become beset by a condition that Jane called academic cowardice. So flattered were they to have been granted access by Mrs. Eliot, they feared that revealing what really was in manuscripts would alienate Mrs. Eliot from them, or worse, alert her attorneys at Faber and Faber. Thanks to the royalties from the worldwide hit musical *Cats* based on one of Eliot's poems, Mrs. Eliot and Faber and Faber could afford a legal dream team virtually unheard of among poetry publishing houses and would frighten scholars with the threat of legal action if anything displeased them.

Fearing their universities would not back them up legally if the reputation of the university was jeopardized by a pending legal action from an undepletable source, scholars whispered and gossiped and cursed about Mrs. Eliot during drinks and dinners at conferences, but praised her incessantly when behind a podium in front of the audience at the same conferences.

Jane scoured through the unpublished letters looking for the word "suppress" again. She found it and instantly knew why that word had stuck in her mind. In the letter written to Pound on November 17, 1939, Eliot ordered Pound twice to suppress anything he had written earlier as a young man. When he wrote the word "suppress", he misspelled it and used capital letters to emphasize more what he expressed in the rest of the letter: that he would do everything in his power to prevent Pound from revealing anything from his earlier work. Here again, Eliot capitalized the verbs in full.

But, what event, thought Jane, had turned such deeply felt gratitude in 1915 into threats by the 1930s?

Then it struck Jane. 1922 was the event, the big event, the publication of *The Waste Land*. Jane had always instinctively felt uneasy about that poem. As a student and later definitely as a writer, she knew no single poet could master so many distinct voices singlehandedly without outside help. She knew from her research that Eliot did not admit the influence the late-nineteenth century British poets had had on him until just before his death. This realization made Jane suspect that he would not admit contemporary influences, let alone help, either.

She didn't have a copy of *The Waste Land* manuscript facsimile with her at the abbey and knew she still had an hour to check it out of the university library. She knew from her copy at home there was a synopsis of how the manuscript was discovered and how it eventually came to be published. She would waste time if she rushed off to the library now. Look at the letters, she thought. Look at the letters, published and unpublished.

There was an unpublished letter with no date on it. The published version had June 1920 in brackets, but again, how could one be sure? It looked like Eliot and Pound were discussing some kind of business deal in the letter. The next unpublished letter she had was dated "22nd December, 1924" and was addressed to Pound in Rapallo. Jane had seen parts of this letter in another book where Pound had apparently pointed out to Eliot that he was indebted to the nineties poets, the same ones Jane had connected to Eliot and Pound alike. Eliot's response was a vehement denial with *The Critierion* letterhead. Eliot was already a voice of authority just two years after the publication of *The Waste Land* and it was clear he no longer needed Pound.

Jane knew she could not stop now, so she moved to the published letters which was the only way she could fill in the gaps up through 1922. It was clear that something had happened after that from the unpublished letters, and which probably held the secret as to why those letters were still unpublished. Jane knew from her research, too, that it was not until 1968, after the chance discovery of *The Waste Land* manuscripts in John Quinn's niece's attic in New York, that the world had come to know that Pound had edited *The Waste Land*. John Quinn was the New York attorney who had collected literary manuscripts and sponsored many literary activities and prizes. Pound had edited the manuscript so rigorously, he renamed the poem from Eliot's original "He Do the Police in Six Voices". In Jane's view, which she had established from her research, Pound had attempted to peel away the overriding presence of John Davidson in *The Waste Land* by radically crossing out a number of pages of the poem where echoes of Davidson were too overt. Davidson was one of the Scottish poets writing about London who Eliot admitted just before his death still haunted him. Davidson, like Eliot, came from a line of fiery Protestant preachers from new nineteenth-century denominations that had their roots in staunchly judgmental Presbyterianism.

But before 1968, the world had not even known that Pound had had a hand in *The Waste Land*. Everyone had still assumed it was the work of a sole poet and for some reason never questioned this, while Eliot never gave credit where credit was due. What was clear after *The Waste Land*, too, was that Pound's life quickly demised into utter shambles. Pound's demise was largely due to his own actions. However, the recent, tragic events in Jane's life made her realize that other people can have as much hand in one's rise as in one's demise.

Jane looked at the published letters that chronicled Pound's and Eliot's collaboration on *The Waste Land*. Jane looked at one letter from Pound to Eliot dated "24 Saturnus An 1" or "24 December 1921" as the editor had pointed out. Pound advises Eliot where to put a few "superfluities". Pound tells Eliot that if he must use them, he should put them at the beginning, not the end of the poem. Pound also dictates that the poem begins with "April is the cruellest month" and ends with "Shantih, shantih, shantih" and should not be longer than the nineteen pages which is how the poem is known now.

If Pound's hand was so crucial to the identity of the poem, where does mere editing end and collaboration begin? Jane thought.

Then Pound moves on by including two poems that Eliot had requested previously. Pound also adds he should include them in a collected edition somewhere, but if he tacked them onto the nineteen pages, it would be a burdensome "wrong note". Obviously, Pound thought they were going to be included somewhere. The poems quickly revealed why. The jocular poems, often a trademark between poets in their letters to each other, each specify both poets' roles in *The Waste Land*.

The first poem, "Sage Homme" clearly divulges Pound's role:

> "These are the Poems of Eliot
> By the Uranian Muse begot;"

Oh, thought Jane, so everybody knew he was gay. Uranian was the practice of homosexuality among male intellectuals in late-nineteenth century London in addition to their heterosexual marriages. Many thought by imitating the intellectuals of ancient Greece, they could attain the intellectuality of ancient Greece.

The poem continued:

> "A Man their Mother was,
> A Muse their Sire.
>
> How did the printed Infancies result
> From Nuptuals thus doubly difficult?
>
> If you must needs enquire
> Know diligent Reader
> That on each Occasion
> Ezra performed the caesarean Operation."

Jane read no further. If this poem had been included, Pound's role in *The Waste Land* would have been known to the world immediately. This letter had not been published until 1988 under the auspices of Valerie Eliot. It was also in the Houghton Library, one of the most rigorously guarded collections in the Eliot stratosphere. Jane knew an Eliot scholar who had by chance been given the wrong box at the Houghton which contained Eliot's unpublished letters and manuscripts. When she had the manuscripts in front of her, she, too, like Jane at Yale, kept it to herself. However, when the librarians at Harvard discovered their mistake, they rushed over to the scholar and yanked the box and the manuscripts out from under her discerning eyes in front of all the other scholars. How different had the response been that Jane got at Yale.

The second poem contained Pound's own analysis of his work. His analysis may explain parts of *The Waste Land* that are so un-Eliotesque, Jane thought. The Decadent, Yeatsian, Grecian elements of Pound's work were clearly admitted in the poem as if Pound wanted to express his indebtedness to the makers of his own poetic voice.

Looking back at the first poem, Jane glanced at what Pound said about Eliot in the rest of the poem. Here, Pound described what she always felt was more Eliotesque, too. The dourness, the disease and the demise which in her view he had developed from a group of late nineteenth century British poets who were distinctly different from the ones who had influenced Pound, but who essentially shared the same aesthetics.

Jane moved on to the next letter dated again by the editor in brackets "[24? January 1922]". This letter, too, was contained in the Houghton Library. "London" was written in brackets at the top of the letter, which indicated the editor assumed it was written from London. Again, no one could be sure. The entire letter was a debate with Pound about what to keep, what to use, what to change, or suggestions about what they might change. As a writer, Jane knew this was collaboration and one of their subjects of debate proved that this is what both of them assumed, too.

Eliot suggested to Pound:

"3. Wish to use Caesarean operation in italics in front.

4. Certainly omit miscellaneous pieces. **Those at end**"

It was clear that, at least at this stage in the life of the poem, Eliot considered Pound as much of a contributor to the poem as he himself. The last line of the letter revealed that Eliot was also looking for publishers on behalf of both of them. Eliot informed Pound that he had written to Scofield Thayer at the literary magazine *The Dial* asking him what he could offer for the poem.

Jane went back and looked at the letter Eliot had written to Thayer on January 20, 1922. In it, he told Thayer that he had a long poem ready:

"It will have been three times through the sieve by Pound as well as myself so should be in final form."

At least initially, Eliot was contacting potential publishers and mentioning both his and Pound's part in the making of the poem.

Jane's intellectual pursuits had caused her to miss dinner at the abbey. Worried that she would be questioned about her absence, Jane decided to resort to the illness excuse as she slipped out the front door to grab a sandwich at a local shop. She took the book of published letters and the facsimile of *The Waste Land* with her because she knew she was on to something and could not stop now.

Seated at the sandwich shop, which in Belgium could only be found in cities full of students where the clientele was penniless but still needed to eat even if it wasn't a true, proper Belgian meal, Jane continued perusing the letters. She read Pound's reply to Eliot written, according to the editor, on January 27, 1922.

Jane was struck by three elements of the letter. The first one was how Pound discussed that he thought he had crossed out one of his wife's, Dorothy's, comments but apparently didn't. Jane never knew that Dorothy Pound had seen the poem, too, and commented on it as Vivien Eliot had. For some reason, Jane had a feeling she should remember this.

The second element that struck Jane was the continued collaboration between Eliot and Pound. It was clear to Jane that for both poets alike, they considered this poem their offspring.

And then the third element struck Jane. It was again a reference to the jocular poem that confessed both Pound's and Eliot's joint efforts in the birth of the poem:

"Do as you like about my obstetric effort."

At this point it was clear to Jane that Pound assumed he and Eliot were going to publish the poem together. This would explain the extreme change in tone in their letters after 1922. It was not until 1968 that the world discovered that the poem had not been the sole effort of T.S. Eliot. By that time, it was too late. Pound was a pariah because of his work for Mussolini during World War II and his subsequent incarceration as a traitor by the United States government. And by that time, Pound was near death.

Eliot had been dead for three years, but he had gone to his grave celebrated as a genius, the quintessential poet of the twentieth century, most notably because of *The Waste Land*.

In Eliot's next published letter to Ezra Pound, Jane found what she needed in order to show that, initially, Eliot had carried the guise that he and Pound were going to publish the poem together, though the outcome was drastically different than the intent. Eliot wrote to Pound on March 12, 1922, angrily after a disappointing offer from Scofield Thayer:

"...and I think it is an outrage that we should be paid less merely because Thayer thinks we will take less and be thankful for it, and I thought somebody ought to take steps to point this out."

Eliot used the pronoun "we" when reporting back to Pound on his negotiations with potential publishers. Pound must have assumed Eliot was negotiating on behalf of both of them. To be sure, Jane went back to Eliot's letter to Scofield Thayer from early 1922 where he mentioned *The Waste Land* had been through the sieve three times by Pound as well as himself. She read the paragraph that led up to that sentence, "I shall shortly have ready a poem of about four hundred and fifty lines, in four parts, and I should like to know whether the *Dial* wishes to print it (not to appear in any periodical on this side) and so quickly as I shall postpone all arrangements for publication until I hear. It could easily divide to go into four issues, if you like, but not more."

When Eliot corresponded with Pound about negotiations with publishers, he used the pronoun "we", but when he corresponded with the publishers themselves, he always used the pronoun "I" with only a passing mention of Pound's contribution. Wait a minute, Jane thought, this would explain the animosity in the letters after 1922 if Eliot had not kept his word to Pound. This would also explain why Valerie Eliot had not yet published those letters and why she, like Eliot before her, kept a tight control on everything.

But there was a lawyer involved, Jane thought. What was his name again? She knew his name was mentioned in the account of the discovery of the manuscripts in the introduction of the facsimile of *The Waste Land*. She couldn't look it up in the introduction to the facsimile, but saw it in the letters, Eliot's attorney in New York was named John Quinn. *The Waste Land* manuscripts had eventually been inherited by Quinn's niece and were not discovered until the early 1950s. The discovery was not revealed to Valerie Eliot, Ezra Pound and the general public at large until 1968. Jane decided to look at the letters addressed to Quinn and Pound. She had a nagging suspicion that there was a discrepancy in what Eliot wrote to Quinn and Pound, just as there was a discrepancy in what Eliot wrote to potential publishers and Pound.

Jane pulled out a pen and a sheet of paper and itemized what Eliot's correspondence to Quinn and Pound had been from mid-1922.

> June 25, 1922: Eliot gives Quinn power of attorney to negotiate with publishers on the publication of *The Waste Land*.

> June 27, 1922: Vivien Eliot writes to Pound about her illness and tells him Eliot has cabled Quinn asking him to take over negotiations with publishers. Quinn has accepted, she writes further. Eliot intercepts this letter and at the end in his own handwriting talks about how inadequate his wife is due to her illness.

Jane made the note next to this entry, "Another Eliot handwritten note at the end of a letter. Ominous."

> July 9, 1922: Eliot writes Pound saying he is still waiting to hear from Quinn about the contract. He does not specify that Quinn has full power of attorney in any instance in the letter.

Jane made a note next to this entry. "Eliot possibly stalling?"

> July 19, 1922: Eliot writes Quinn and offers him *The Waste Land* manuscripts.
> July 19, 1922: Eliot writes Pound and mentions nothing about *The Waste Land*. Only in the last line does Eliot mention he hopes Quinn is making progress.

Jane made this note: "Same day, two different stories."

> July 28, 1922: Eliot writes Pound that there are two copies of *The Waste Land* (one copy has gone to Quinn and the other is in Eliot's possession) and assures Pound he will let him have a copy as soon as he can make one.

Jane noted, "Stalling?"

Jane skimmed through all the letters after this letter. She found an interesting one sent to one of the co-owners of the *Dial*, the American magazine *The Waste Land* was first published in simultaneously with the British literary magazine *The Criterion*. She noted the date and the recipient.

> August 15, 1922: Eliot writes James Watson, co-owner of the
> *Dial*, suggesting he be awarded the annual *Dial* award for *The
> Waste Land* in order to increase sales.

Jane scribbled, "At no point does Eliot mention Pound's contribution to the poem."

> August 21, 1922: Eliot to Quinn, accepts contract.
> August 30, 1922: Eliot to Pound, (insulting tone, includes insulting quotes from poetry) ensuring Pound all his notes, letters and cables will be included and paid for. Informs him about the prize and asks why they didn't give it to Pound, but that he was not going to bother Quinn about it again.
> September 21, 1922: Eliot sends manuscripts with Pound's edits to Quinn.

At this point, Jane knew enough. The tone of the letters deteriorated even more from there and more and more of Eliot's handwritten threats and insults accumulated for Pound as time went on. Then, one of Eliot's last letters of 1922 was addressed to John Quinn, dated December 27th.

> "Thank you very much for your kind letter of the 4th. It contained a filing card from the Copyright Office of the Library of Congress, certifying that *The Waste Land* was Copyright in my name."

With these words, Pound's fate had been sealed. And with this discovery, Jane could hear Eliot's voice ringing in her head with his most infamous quote which previously had caused so much conjecture, but now for Jane contained so much certainty.

"Immature poets imitate. Mature poets steal."

Only she knew somebody had to believe her.

"Hurry up please. It's time."

Stunned to hear what seemed like a voice from *The Waste Land*, Jane looked up deer-eyed from shock and up from her book at the English waiter who stood before her. Frazzled, she answered, "Oh yes, of course, my apologies," and stood up to leave with her fingers in the two pages in the book where she had left off. As she walked quickly, just cantering on a run, through the medieval alleyways and cobblestone streets back to the abbey in the twilight, cathedrals towering over her, she rushed through the front doors of the abbey to her cubbyhole room. She quickly called Professor Stanford.

"Professor Stanford?"

"Yes?"

"It's Jane. I think I've stumbled onto something. You know how I have Eliot's unpublished letters to Pound from Yale and I showed you how derogatory the tone is even though their letters had been amicable before?"

"Yes?"

"Well, I think I figured it out."

"Yes?"

"Eliot and Pound were going to publish *The Waste Land* together but Eliot made off with the manuscripts and sent them to his lawyer in New York."

There was silence on the other end of the conversation.

"You know I have a conference in Utrecht in a few weeks. Should I discuss this? I've discussed my earlier work so often…"

"No." Professor Stanford cut her off. "No."

After Jane and Professor Stanford hung up, she quickly called Dr. Ungaro to get a second opinion about mentioning it at the upcoming conference. Her answer was as curt and forthcoming as Professor Stanford's answer.

"No, Jane. By no means must you mention this. No."

"But what…"

"No, Jane, don't do it. It's your work, you must protect it."

And with her discovery that evening and these phone conversations, Professor Stanford and Dr. Ungaro had given her the best academic advice any advisor could. Eliot had originally been an academic. Theft was a trick of the trade.

Jane had been forced to return home because her husband had blocked their accounts. Though she knew it was not safe for her at home, she longed to be closer to her children to protect them, though she also feared that since her husband's violence toward her was so explosive, it could instantly be redirected toward their daughters. Jane knew she had to go to the police to report his latest abuse and she also knew she needed to hire an attorney to initiate divorce proceedings.

Jane paid off everything she owed at the abbey and drove home with just enough gas to make the two and a half hour trip. Her dad had wired her some emergency cash so that she could open her own bank account that her husband could not access. Once she was home, she slept in the bathroom because she could lock the door. Jane didn't think sleeping with the children would deter his violence since he had abused her without any scruples in front of them. Their presence did not bring him to reason before, and because she had awoken in the morning a few times with him standing over her since his physical abuse had begun, she did not want to put the children at risk in any way by being physically too close to her, especially while they were sleeping.

At the same time, this decision broke her heart because she longed to hold her children and protect them, but she knew following her mothering instincts could endanger them more because she was the object of his explosive violence and rage. Jane knew Lisa and Danielle longed for her to hold them, too, especially at night, but Jane also feared that if Lisa and Danielle showed any loyalty to her, it would unleash her husband's wrath against them, too.

That day, Jane knew she had to take care of two things while her children were at school and her husband was at work. Jane knew she had to file a complaint with the police before her bruises faded from her husband's latest attack, and she had to get an attorney.

When she got to the police station, the officer behind the counter asked why she was here.

"I'm here to file a domestic violence complaint."

"When did it happen?"

"Two days ago."

"Why didn't you come earlier?" the officer yelled back at her.

"Because I had to get away from him first before it got worse, now I need to file a complaint before the bruises heal. This is the end of my marriage, I know. I nearly filed a complaint before, so this time I wanted to think clearly before I took this step because it's not an easy decision."

"Now it's your word against his because you didn't come right away! There's nothing we can do for you now."

"I want to file a complaint and have these bruises photographed for evidence."

The officer's patience was wearing thin and Jane wanted to keep him on her side even though she knew she couldn't let him just send her away. "Then I'll have to schedule an appointment for you. The earliest is next week."

"What about the bruises then? They'll be healed by then and you won't have any evidence."

"You need to make an appointment with the forensic doctor in Lelystad and he'll have to examine you and file a report with your complaint."

"Do you have a number I can call to make an appointment with them?"

"No, you'll have to look it up yourself."

Jane's spirits sunk. All those campaigns about domestic violence being a priority were just window dressing. "When is my appointment to file a complaint?" She opened her diary to pencil it in.

"Next Tuesday at 11:00."

"That's fine." Jane wrote it down while the officer typed it in the computer. "Thank you," and Jane turned to leave the station. She decided she should go straight to her family doctor's office so that he could get the injuries on record now. Hopefully, his office also had the number of the forensic doctor's office so that she wouldn't have to go to the library to look up the number. While her kids were at school, she didn't want to be home alone in case her husband suddenly came home early from work. Her family doctor got her in during his emergency appointment hour and put the injuries and their cause in her medical records. The receptionist found the number of the forensic doctor for her. She called their office from her family doctor's office.

"The first appointment I have for you is next week."

"But the bruises will have healed by then. My husband attacked me two days ago."

"I'm sorry, that's the earliest I have for you."

"But then there won't be any evidence of the abuse. I'm at my family doctor's office now. They can confirm that for you."

"There's nothing I can do."

The medical receptionist went and got Jane's family doctor. He told Jane to give her the phone. "This is Dr. Jansen. My patient needs to be examined today so that there is enough forensic evidence for a possible prosecution. I know the forensic examiner and if you don't make an appointment this afternoon for her, I will call him myself and arrange an appointment for her so that she has his report to file her complaint with the police. This woman is a victim. Who are you protecting by following due process? The victim or the abuser?"

"My apologies, Dr. Jansen. I can get her in at 2:15 this afternoon."

At the forensic examiner's office, Jane broke down and cried after the examination was over as he handed her the report with a circle around the left breast to indicate the location of the now yellowing bruise. "I'm so ashamed," she told the examiner through her tears. "I'm about to get my PhD in literature, but I didn't see the classic story."

"Stay in contact with your family doctor through this process. He's a good guy. Take good care of yourself and your children."

"Thank you. I will. Goodbye."

"Goodbye."

Jane spent the next few days trying to find an attorney. Five law offices turned her down and she could not pinpoint the reason. One office made an appointment and Jane went in and assumed the proceedings would start because the lawyer gave her specific instructions about what to do and not to do. The next morning, another attorney at the same law firm called and said they would not be taking on her case. When she asked why, the attorney did not want to give her an answer.

Jane eventually found another attorney a few days later, but Jane's instincts told her that this attorney could not be trusted. For now, Jane had no other choice.

A colleague of Professor Stanford's had advised Jane to present at this conference since an important Modernist scholar was going to be there. Jane had run into him in the hallway in Louvain just after Professor Stanford had told her she needed to look into her DNA.

"There's still an opening for a PhD candidate's paper. I can put you down for a presentation."

"I don't know if I have anything new to present," Jane mumbled, still trying to come to terms with the meeting she had just had with Professor Stanford.

"Jane, you need to be there. Just send me a generic title." With that gentle order, Jane was committed.

The date of the conference was upon her and after waking stiffly on the bathroom floor, she readied her children for school after her husband left early for work. She then caught the train to Utrecht, wondering what she was going to present since she couldn't present what she had recently discovered, but knew she was going to be grilled because she wasn't presenting anything new. The carbuncular comparative literature professor was chairing her session. It was rumored he had cherry-picked all the PhD candidates who would be presenting while the Modernist scholar was there to make sure only candidates presented who cited his work and looked up to him, but he came one presenter short. Louvain, which was co-sponsoring the conference, demanded he include one of their PhD candidates, but the university did not tell him who. Since Jane was the only candidate doing research on Modernism, she was the natural presenter from Louvain. Unbeknownst to Jane, a professor from Leiden who had helped get Jane published in 2005 offered to give up his presentation spot in case the comparative literature professor protested when he found out who was presenting from Louvain. The organizers from Louvain and Leiden hoped the comparative literature professor would not openly protest Jane's presentation in front of an internationally-acclaimed visitor; however, they could never be sure and decided to have a back-up plan just in case.

Jane took the copies of the letters with her from Yale, just in case she got to talk to the Modernist scholar alone. Jane was not going to tell her everything, but at least let her know that she had unpublished letters to Pound after 1922. Even if Jane's research wasn't interesting to the scholar, the manuscripts would be. Jane didn't know why, but she also brought a copy of her father's birth certificate which had "W.C. Williams" registered as the attending physician at her father's birth. Her mother had brought it along during her last visit. Jane had fished it out of some old papers and now included it with the manuscripts for safe keeping.

Jane's paper was the last one of the day, which gave her time to sneak to the university library and make a few copies of Doré's engravings of London with their circular patterns and his illustrations for Dante's Hell.

This was further evidence Jane had gathered in the past few years to support her argument that the artistic and poetic strategies that Eliot had used had been commonplace as much as fifty years earlier. If she showed this, then possibly it would take some of the sting out of the comparative literature professor's inevitable grilling.

When it came time for Jane to give her paper, she decided to have some fun with it. Although she couldn't tell everything she knew, she could give her research an aura of suspense. If Eliot had stolen from Pound, hadn't he really stolen from the late-nineteenth century poets, too? Jane decided she wouldn't mention Pound at all to avoid discussions about Pound's fascist sympathies with the comparative literature professor. Realistically, she knew she would get a discussion during her paper with him anyway at some point because he hated Eliot and anything that had to do with him. Bringing Pound into the discussion would just add fuel to the fire and the comparative literature professor could then accuse Jane of having fascist tendencies because she respected Pound's work. Jane was familiar with tactics such as his; when he knew he could not win the argument, he would try and make Jane look like a pariah.

Jane read some poems from the British poets and then Eliot's poems that resembled them the most. Then she read examples from Dante and Baudelaire to show that the British poets of the late-nineteenth century were using the same aesthetics. The word "aesthetics" was the word that set the comparative literature professor off right in front of the visiting Modernist scholar.

"What do you mean with aesthetics? We're not going to discuss individual poets here! We are discussing theories and movements which are larger than individual poets!"

"Yes, professor. But you must substantiate theories and discussions about artistic and literary movements with evidence from individual texts that are ultimately written and created by individual poets."

*Over London – By Rail*
*London: A Pilgrimage, Gustave Doré and Blanchard Jerrold, 1872.*

*Newgate – Exercise Yard*
*London: A Pilgrimage. Gustave Doré and Blanchard Jerrold, 1872.*

*The Lustful*
*Dante Aligieri's Gottliche Komödie… Illustrirt von Gustave Doré, 1861.*

*The Hypocrites*
*Dante Aligieri's Gottliche Komödie… Illustrirt von Gustave Doré, 1861.*

"We are not going to discuss individual poets here!" the professor repeated. Jane noticed he did not mention Eliot by name because he knew the visiting Modernist scholar was a great fan of Eliot and had published a number of articles on Eliot's work. She, too, was a theorist like Jane's advisor, Professor Stanford. However, like Professor Stanford, she recognized the importance of including aesthetics in discussions about literary theory.

"With all due respect, professor, if you give me a chance to finish my paper, you will see that I base my research on Genette's theory of inter-textuality."

"We are here to discuss theories of Modernism, not individual poets!" this time he screamed and the vehemence of his insolence was already making him the pariah. Jane decided to seal his fate.

Jane rose her hand just above the table she was sitting at and pointed her finger at him. "That is dogma, not debate!"

The room fell silent and the carbuncular comparative literature professor pursed his lips, frozen in his silence without a rebuttal or a refute to the accusation of being an unyielding authoritarian which his generation never expected to become. Ultimately, his silence lasted too long and he conceded.

"Yes, it's dogma." The silence ensued again.

Jane quietly looked down at her paper and then up again at the visiting scholar who nodded her approval at Jane, overtaking the outwitted chair of the session, which gave Jane the implied signal, too, that she should continue with her paper.

Jane cleared her throat and continued. "Eliot's silence on his British predecessors is curious, not only because it redirected the spotlight on him continuously after their work was no longer published, a situation which may have been exasperated by the fact that the man who was later to become Eliot's attorney, John Quinn of New York, also bought most of the British poets' manuscripts during the early twentieth century until his death in 1924. Pound..."

The comparative literature professor gaffed and turned his head. The visiting scholar held up her hand to silence him and looked at Jane to give her the signal to continue.

"Pound questioned American collectors' almost insatiable appetite for these manuscripts in an article in 1915 and Quinn responded with an angry letter to Pound that Pound's article referred to him. As time went on and especially after the publication of *The Waste Land*, which Quinn helped facilitate the publication of extensively in 1922, not only had Eliot's immediate British predecessors faded away in comparison to Eliot, but also Eliot's contemporaries. This sequence of circumstances is not based on Eliot's talent alone, and in fact, Pound protested in a letter in December 1924 to Eliot that he did not admit the influence the poets of the late-nineteenth century had had on him."

"How did you see those letters? Eliot's letters after 1922 are unpublished and you need permission to see them. Did Valerie Eliot give you permission to see them?" the visiting scholar demanded of Jane.

"I got a grant to the Beinecke at Yale. They're not as strict there as the other libraries."

"You're presenting this like a plot," the scholar replied.

"Maybe it is. You'll have to wait for my PhD." With that reply, the whole room let out a gasp of air, revealing their disappointment.

The comparative literature professor called a bathroom break to curtail his frustration, but Jane told him her paper was finished, so if he wanted to end the session, he could and then everyone could proceed to drinks and dinner. Jane took all her papers and notes with her and, of course, the manuscripts and went and stood in the line in front of the ladies' room. The visiting scholar got in line behind her. Jane courteously let her go in front of her and everyone else who lined up so that she and the visiting scholar could confer in the ladies' room with no one else around, especially the comparative literature professor. The visiting scholar caught Jane's cue and let everyone else cut in front of her, too. Then, after the visiting scholar and Jane had attended nature's call and washed their hands, the visiting scholar dried her hands and said, "Show me what you've got."

Jane pulled out the letters from the Beinecke. The scholar saw the envelope and the paper with Yale's symbol and the Beinecke's copyright notification on the backs of the sheets of paper.

"You've got manuscripts from the Beinecke? How did you get them?"

"I just went there and they copied them for me. I have a number of unpublished letters to Pound here after 1922, but I've also found discrepancies between some of the published letters and what is in the original from before 1922."

"Does Valerie Eliot know you have this? Did she give you permission to see them?"

"No, but she did answer my request for permission with a question about whether I wanted to quote from any of the manuscripts."

"Her usual response, even if you do get one. Do you have her letter with you?"

Jane nodded.

"Let me see it."

Jane showed the scholar the letter with the megalomaniac signature. "Oh God," the scholar grunted, "She uses that signature everywhere. She's just a secretary, that's why he married her! Her secretary's loyalty towards him is so naive, it borders on stupidity. Show me the discrepancies in the texts."

As Jane started to shuffle through the copies of the original letters to find the one she was looking for, the envelope with her father's birth certificate slipped onto the floor. The scholar bent to pick it up for Jane. "Oh, I'm so sorry," Jane said.

The scholar reached for the envelope. She noticed it was addressed to an address in Rutherford, New Jersey. "What is this? Who do you know in Rutherford?" The scholar had also published extensively on Williams.

"My dad was born and raised there. That's his birth certificate. William Carlos Williams delivered him and was his and my grandparents' doctor while he was growing up. My grandmother was an English teacher and deacon at the church across from Williams' house and practice. I was baptized there."

The scholar rose up and handed Jane the yellowed envelope and stared at Jane intently. "Could I see the birth certificate, please?"

"Why, yes, of course." Jane managed to put the manuscripts down across the bathroom sinks while she supported them on her thigh by standing on the ball of her raised left foot. Now that her hands were as free as she could get them under the circumstances, she opened the envelope. The scholar read over the yellowed document, which stated:

"DIVISION OF VITAL STATISTICS
BUREAU OF HEALTH
CITY OF PASSAIC, NEW JERSEY
CERTIFICATE OF BIRTH REGISTRATION
THIS CERTIFIES that a certificate of birth has been filed in this department bearing the name of David Elliot Hooper who was born on January 3rd, 1935 at General Hospital.
Name of father Raymond Renaldo Hooper
Maiden / name of mother Doris Benham Hussey
Name of attendant at birth W.C. Williams, MD
A.D. Bolton
Registrar of Vital Statistics"

The scholar folded the envelope up carefully and ever so slowly and returned the birth certificate to the equally yellow envelope. She raised her eyes and stared at Jane intently, though not threatening at all, and handed her the envelope in a respective silence. When Jane accepted the envelope back and had put it safely under her right thumb that cradled the manuscripts together with her fingers underneath them, and safely in the cup of the palm of her hand, the scholar gently commanded her, "Show me what you have on Eliot."

Jane proceeded to show the visiting scholar the insults and threats to Pound after 1922 which Eliot always sent on *The Criterion* and Faber and Faber letterhead that she had bookmarked with her fingers. Then Jane showed the scholar the largest discrepancy between the published letters and the original letter. A letter dated February 2, 1915, from Eliot to Pound, mentioning that one poem was included, was not present in the original letter, in fact no poem was present in the original letter, yet one had been included in the published version. In the notes to the published letter, it was mentioned that the poem came from the Berg Collection at the New York Public Library which had been purchased from Quinn's descendants.

Jane explained this to the scholar and added, "If Eliot was threatening Pound not to release any of his early work that Pound still had in his possession as late as the 1930s, and Valerie Eliot won't publish the letters after 1922, and even if she does, no one will get permission to see the originals or the manuscripts, are we supposed to just take her word for it that this is the poem Eliot sent to Pound? It was found in a completely different location in New York and is part of a completely different collection. Pound kept everything with him until his death in Italy in 1971 and now almost everything is at the Beinecke at Yale. It's not a coincidence that he didn't give them to Harvard where Eliot's family has so much influence."

The scholar looked down and turned her head, "You've got something there. You're on to something. Don't stop now. Are you going to dinner?"

"Yes."

The scholar picked up her purse and strung it over her shoulder. "Let me go ahead of you." The scholar grabbed Jane's upper arm and squeezed it slightly. "Have you looked at Williams' poetry at all?"

"No, I'm trying to get this research on Eliot and Pound done first."

"You need to."

Jane's left leg started to tremble from balancing the manuscripts for so long on the ball of her foot where the bathroom sink ended. "The timing isn't right."

"Jane, you're a mother, too, aren't you?"

"Yes, I am."

"Then you should know that the timing is never right, but the work still must be done. Look into Williams, oh, and make sure you invite Valerie Eliot to your viva. Vivas are public here, aren't they?" The scholar winked at Jane and smiled while she let go of Jane's upper arm. The scholar turned to leave the bathroom and Jane gathered the letters, manuscripts and birth certificate as orderly as she could. She was relieved everyone had left the university building, but she also knew security would soon be combing the building to get the literary loiterers out. At least the famous scholar was still there to vouch for her.

As she pushed open the ladies' room door, the scholar turned and advised Jane, "Make sure you have some fun tonight at dinner. Something tells me it may be awhile before you have fun again."

Jane turned her head to the scholar and smiled sheepishly, still performing her balancing act. "Ok, I will. Or at least, I'll try."

"Good. Dante writes that good memories carry us through terrible times."

Jane nodded in acquiescence and looked down. The scholar let the door shut behind her with a bang and returned Jane to her solitude.

O foolish girl!
Listen to your mothers well!
Trust their experience and be wary of the wrath to come!

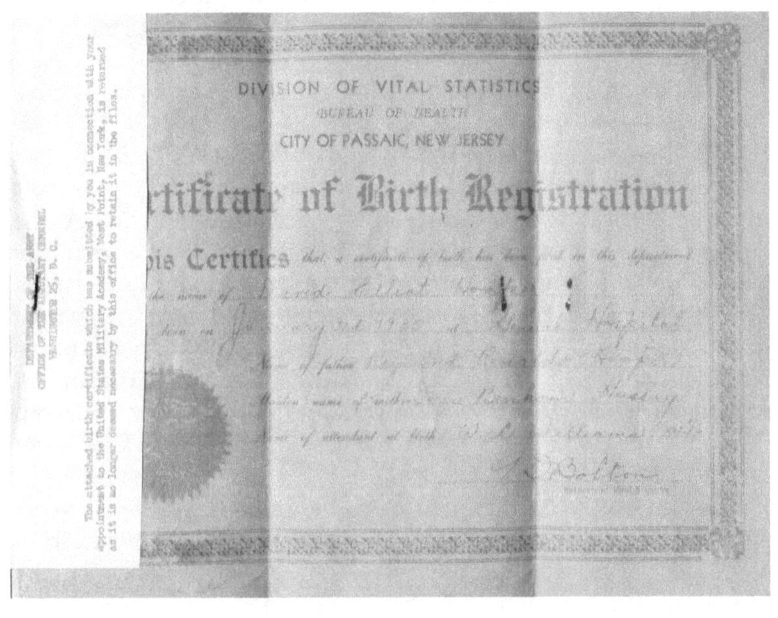

*David Elliot Hooper's birth certificate with William Carlos Williams recorded as the attending physician at the birth.*

Jane entered the restaurant where dinner was being held and, heavily laden with the weights of Modernist literature, she ran into Dr., soon to be professor, Lebenstein just beyond the door, handing over his coat to the student working the cloak room.

"There you are!" he exclaimed. Jane had never experienced him so exuberant before. She assumed he had had something to drink.

"Oh, hi!"

"Can I help you with something? We can't have you going in there looking like a bag lady, can we?"

"No." Jane was completely taken aback by this comment. She had lived on the Continent for years, but still could not anticipate their rudeness, since she was only carrying a purse and a laptop case. As she put her purse and her laptop case down and took off her coat, she knew if she didn't let him carry something, he would get suspicious. On the other hand, Jane didn't feel too comfortable about him getting so close to the manuscripts, but she couldn't let him carry her purse. As a man, he would never do that. She handed her coat to the student running the cloak room and asked Dr. Lebenstein to carry her laptop case while she kept a sharp eye on it. There was no way he knew what she had with her, anyway.

They got to the bar first and Dr. Lebenstein asked, "Shall we sit down here and have a drink?" As usual, they would be removed from the rest of the crowd which had gathered in the bar area closer to the restaurant. Jane wondered whether these things ever dawned on Dr. Lebenstein. Frankly, she doubted he had the slightest idea what sitting separately from the rest of the group would suggest. But she went along with it anyway because a major Modernist compatriot scholar had just advised her to have some fun.

They both sat down with a glass of wine. "So how are things in Louvain?"

"The food's better. Professor Stanford would probably add that the mood is better there, too."

Dr. Lebenstein laughed. "The Dutch-Flemish rivalry will never cease!"

"I guess not."

"How have you been? I mean you, your husband and your girls."

"I'm getting a divorce."

"What?"

"Yeah, he started beating me up when I transferred to Louvain."

"What? Oh my God, Jane! How are the girls?"

"It's an awful situation. He's facing battery charges, but he can't be evicted until the divorce proceedings have started and a judge orders him out of the house if he doesn't agree to leave on his own. I sleep on the bathroom floor so that I can lock the door and not endanger the girls if I sleep with them. The three of us live in fear. Finding a lawyer has been hard, too. They don't like domestic violence cases."

"What? I would think it would spur a good lawyer's sense of justice."

"I agree, but I'm still looking for that lawyer. I've got one now that will make do for the time being, but she's the only one who would take me. Because it's a domestic violence case, I'm the victim and I'm on legal aid. I'm keeping my eye out for a better lawyer, though. As soon as I catch her in a mistake, I'm dropping her. These cases remain exhaustive after the divorce is over because the perpetrator of the violence tries to control his ex-wife through custody laws and so he continues to abuse her through the court system. After the divorce, he still has an income so he can afford continuing court proceedings, while she's usually on welfare and her legal aid has run out."

"Couldn't you go back to the States?"

"No. Then I'd be an international child abductor."

"But you're an American citizen and so are your children."

"Nationalities aren't important in The Hague Convention on International Child Abduction. It's where the children are habitually residing."

"But he abused you! Isn't that an argument?"

"No. He has to give me permission to leave with the children, but most abusers let the woman leave with the children and then retract their permission and file a child abduction complaint anyway. The judges always side with the father regardless of the underlying circumstances because they don't consider domestic violence against the mother to be a threat to the children. And judges rarely give permission to leave. They consider a move more traumatic than domestic violence."

"But just being around that sort of behavior is dangerous!"

"I know."

"The girls will eventually grow up. Can't they choose then where they want to live?"

"When they're sixteen we can emigrate."

"Jane, that's a jail sentence. How old are they now?"

"Three and five."

"Oh God, Jane. I had no idea."

"Don't worry about it. What can I do? You have to play with the cards you're dealt in life. That's all any of us can do. I probably should tell you something, too. My husband is so jealous to the point of delusion. He suspects that any man I've associated with who has blue eyes may be the father of my children and not him."

"What???" Dr. Lebenstein's crystal blue eyes were wide open now.

"Both of the girls have piercing crystal blue eyes and both his eyes and my eyes are dark brown."

"Well, that can happen, can't it? Are there blue eyes in the family?"

"Oh yeah, on both sides. Both grandmothers have crystal blue eyes. Doctors in the family have even tried to explain to him that it's possible. Brown is the dominant eye color but it doesn't have to work out that way. But, you know, once somebody has an idea in his head, perception is everything."

"Oh God. Do I need to carry a baseball bat?"

Jane smiled weakly. "I don't think it will come to that. But now I understand why he tried to discourage me so many times to pursue my PhD. He felt threatened, but that's his problem, not mine. He can't ask me to give up my dreams because of his insecurities."

"Oh, no. Never give up your dreams for anybody. That's what I tell my daughter, too."

"How is your daughter?"

"Oh, she's fine. She's growing up so fast."

"I heard a few years ago that you were getting a divorce."

"I was."

"But you're still married?"

"Yes, I am. But we live like brother and sister."

"What? You can't live like that! You'll whither from the inside! Why didn't you get a divorce?"

"Everything was final but we couldn't bring ourselves to sign it. I'm not going to stay forever, though. About eight years to go."

"Did you say something about jail sentences?" Jane looked away and took two swallows of wine. Dr. Lebenstein did the same.

"Hey," he looked up. "The whole conference is already seated for dinner."

"They have been for ten minutes."

"There are only seats left at the end of the table across from each other. I guess you're stuck with me, Miss Hooper. Oh, sorry, it's still

Sweens for the time being. Let's go, time for dinner!" He stood up, grabbed his glass of wine and waltzed around her and winked at her while she stood up to catch up with him and followed him to the table. Jane quickly saw why those two seats were left over. The cream of the crop and the visiting scholar were seated at the head of the table and had sat down early, while the grayest of the academic mice filled in the middle of the table. Jane and Dr. Lebenstein got the other end but she knew their neighbors at the table would be so boringly silent, she and Dr. Lebenstein would be able to continue to have some literary fun since he was in good spirits and she was prone to listening to good advice.

All evening long their conversation drifted from literature to philosophy and religion. Since Jane was an American and the Democrats had just secured Congress, foreshadowing the outcome of the next presidential election, they couldn't leave that subject untouched.

Then the conversation drifted back to religion and whether Islam was a peaceful religion. Both Dr. Lebenstein and Jane agreed it was. Then back to literature and Jane's hypothesis that Anna Karenina was more of a woman than Madame Bovary. It was like the rest of the table wasn't there.

"Why do you think that?" Dr. Lebenstein probed.

"Anna Karenina was caught between her own aspirations for her life, which were unacceptable to her husband though many people told him to let her have her divorce and her son. He tried to make her choose. He held her for ransom by keeping her son from her. It's the same kind of inhumane choice the Nazi soldier made Sophie take in *Sophie's Choice*. Anna Karenina was faced with a dilemma analogous to a Greek tragedy." Being a classicist, Dr. Lebenstein's eyes lit up when Jane said this. Jane concluded, "Madame Bovary was only a bored housewife whose daughter was no consequence to her anyway. She would have killed herself regardless."

"Wow, interesting. Most feminists consider them to be equal heroines."

"I disagree. They're vastly different."

"Jane, can I ask you a personal question?"

Jane was taken aback and didn't know how to answer. "Sure."

"Did your husband have any reason to suspect..."

"You mean, are the children his?"

"Well, yeah, but not that completely. I know they are, but..."

"Did I ever show feelings for anyone else that would have made him suspicious? Is that what you're trying to say?'

"Yeah, sort of."

Jane, whose courage had been mustered up by the wine, got bold and said, "Dr. Lebenstein, I love you."

He looked at her, stunned.

"I always have."

Dr. Lebenstein was silenced for a moment and his eyes welled up. "I'm not leaving my wife. I can't just now."

"I have the patience of Bin Ladin."

Dr. Lebenstein choked on the sip of wine he had tried to swallow down after disappointing Jane and had to spit it on the plant next to him. After that he could not contain his laughter while he made excuses to the waiter, trying to wipe down the plant pot and the leaves of the plant that contained the drops of wine mixed with his saliva. Jane could not contain her laughter either as the gray mice turned awry to look at what was causing all the commotion.

The other end of the table looked up over towards Dr. Lebenstein and Jane to see what the waiters were fussing about. The visiting scholar smiled wryly and looked at Jane out of the corner of her eye.

She knew Jane had followed her advice.

Jane's doctor, Dr. Jansen, has asked her to come in at least once a week and check in with his office by phone every day while her husband was still in the house. Jane kept him abreast of everything that was going on.

"So, has he been served the divorce papers yet?"

"No, but that should be any day now. He was furious the other night because the police sent him a letter asking him to come in for questioning regarding a battery complaint."

"Jane, this is when things are most dangerous for the woman and children: when the woman decides to leave the abusive relationship. That's when abusers get desperate because they know they are about to lose control. They resort to equally desperate measures. You've got to be very careful for yourself and your children. Be vigilant at all times."

"Ok. I know."

"I know you can't leave the house because then legally you've forfeited it even if you did leave to flee abuse. I know you can't leave because you may lose the house in the divorce proceedings and the judge will want to keep the children in their parental home, so you've got to stay so that they are kept with you, too." Dr. Jansen was well-versed in Dutch divorce law. He had assisted many women in similar situations since beginning his practice twenty-five years earlier. What astonished him most is that so little had improved for women in Jane's situation since then. "But, God, Jane, be vigilant. Situations like this tend to worsen dramatically around the holiday season."

"Ok."

"Keep sleeping in the bathroom until he's gone."

"Ok."

"One more question. Do you have anything to take your mind off everything?"

"My research."

"But, isn't that putting even more of drain on you mentally? Don't push yourself too far now, Jane," he advised her though he knew full well it was better that she sought escapism in her work right now than in alcohol or any other substance. He just didn't want her to overdo it because he knew the situation was going to get worse before it got better.

"I don't know. I think this whole situation has given me new insights into my work."

"What do you mean?" Dr. Jansen probed her, intrigued.

"Well, the connection between the poetry and human nature." Jane had kept Dr. Jansen posted on everything that had happened personally but also what she had discovered in her research and, of course, what Professor Stanford had advised her to look into regarding her family history. When Dr. Jansen heard what Professor Stanford had told Jane to look into, he wasn't surprised for a second, nor did he doubt Professor Stanford's advice. As a medical doctor, he was enormously intrigued because Williams had been a doctor himself. But he also knew Williams' behavior, his numerous affairs, was more commonplace in his profession than he or any of his colleagues would like to admit.

Dr. Jansen knew, too, that Jane's possible ancestry would help him out greatly when the authorities would inevitably come calling and inquire into Jane's mental state. Jane did not fit the stereotypes for a woman, and especially for a mother, commonly held in Dutch society and by the Dutch authorities. Now Dr. Jansen could say she came from a long line of brilliant people without compromising doctor-patient confidentiality. He knew they would take his word on that over hers and to make sure, he told her emphatically not to discuss her work or her possible family history with anyone, especially the authorities. Dr. Jansen knew that if she did, the authorities would immediately brand her a mental case.

Dr. Jansen had also seen so many times before how quickly the authorities, based on the word of the woman's abuser, would deal her the mental card at the drop of a hat and disregard the man's obvious mentally unstable, violent behavior. Putting his victim in a dark light distracted the authorities from his own behavior. It was an age-old proven defense that the woman had provoked him and therefore deserved the abuse, blaming the victim. Though this excuse was not supposed to be accepted in their decision to pursue a case, the police, the first contact with the judicial system, would often dismiss any battery or sexual assault complaint filed by a female victim at the slightest hint of any mental incapacity on her part. The police continued to do this regardless of overwhelming forensic evidence and a confession from the perpetrator, which was the high burden of proof put on all battery cases whether they were domestic disputes or otherwise. Dr. Jansen knew from his years of experience that nothing had changed for women since he had entered the medical profession. The abusers still had the system on their side because as men they received the greatest benefit of the doubt. This was a universal truth wherever you might find yourself in the world, East or West, North or South. Stereotypes die hard in a man's world.

For these reasons, too, Dr. Jansen wanted to hear more from Jane about her work. He noticed she lit up the most when she talked about two things, her work and her daughters, Lisa and Danielle. "Would you mind elaborating on your findings?" he asked.

"Well, would you mind looking at something for me?" Dr. Jansen nodded. By this time, he had usually looked at his clock, worried about his next patient, but he decided his next patient could wait. "There's something in the published letters that's been bothering me. I heard once about these symptoms Eliot's first wife had, but it wasn't for the condition she says the symptoms are from." Jane pulled the book of Eliot's published letters from her bag. She still carried everything critical to her research with her to keep her husband from confiscating her work and destroying it as she suspected her father-in-law had done with her mother-in-law's master's thesis.

She opened the book to the pages that contained Vivien Eliot's letter to Pound dated June 27, 1922. "Could you take a look at these symptoms? The letter mentions a diagnosis of colitis." She turned the book toward Dr. Jansen and handed it to him and pointed to the symptoms at the top of the page.

Dr. Jansen read them aloud. "A slight, recurrent fever. Swollen glands. Inability to concentrate. Exhaustion. Insomnia. Migraines. They seem to have diagnosed colitis, when that's a symptom itself, sort of off hand."

Dr. Jansen was silent for a moment and looked askance. "These are symptoms of poisoning."

"T.S. Eliot is considered to be the greatest poet of the twentieth century."

"What else do you have on him, Jane?"

"This was the letter Eliot's wife wrote Pound to let him know Eliot had contacted an attorney in New York to negotiate the publication of *The Waste Land*, considered to be the greatest poem of the twentieth century, which Eliot had written and Pound edited at the very least extensively. I've put together the fact that they were going to publish it together but Eliot stole the manuscripts and sent them to this same attorney in New York and gave him full power of attorney to publish the poem and register Eliot's copyright as the sole author. Once that had happened, Pound was powerless and later penniless to do anything. He ended up in Italy, where he did a few radio broadcasts for Mussolini. The Americans invaded, captured him and he was imprisoned as a traitor in Washington for twelve years after the war. Williams and Pound went to university together and Pound mentored Williams as he did Eliot. As a doctor, Williams regularly monitored Pound's condition at the mental hospital, St. Elizabeth's, by driving down to Washington from New Jersey."

"How do you know that, Jane?" Dr. Jansen was surprised she mentioned Williams at all. When she visited Dr. Jansen after returning from Louvain, she expressed her utmost disbelief at what her advisor told her to do and told her doctor how insolent she was with her advisor because it was not the time or place to look into that now. She had her hands full with her divorce and her research into Eliot and Pound.

"I've been looking into Williams' autobiography," she answered, perturbed. "I've always carried a distrust of Eliot. It turns out Williams did, too. I've never thought Eliot was as good a poet as everyone made him out to be."

Dr. Jansen nodded slowly in acquiescence. He caught the sudden irritation in her tone of voice when he asked where she got that information on Williams. Obviously, she couldn't put what her advisor told her in the freezer completely to examine later, but it was clear to him she was taking everything in about Williams in piecemeal, in the small doses at a time she could handle. He decided to redirect the conversation back to Eliot.

"Ok. Back to Eliot. So it seems Pound's reputation was ruined by his political affiliations and his subsequent incarceration in a military mental institution so he was powerless to take on Eliot. With his reputation ruined, no one would have believed him anyway. Do you have more on Eliot and his relationship with his first wife?"

"Eventually he had her institutionalized for mental illness and she spent the rest of her life there. But since you mentioned symptoms of poisoning, you might want to take a look at a letter Eliot wrote to Pound just three weeks later."

Dr. Jansen held the book for a moment and read over something at the end of the letter that caught his eye before he handed it back to Jane. "I see Eliot had something to add at the end of this letter in his own handwriting. Emphasizing how mentally incapacitated his wife really is. It sounds like he may have tried to shed doubt on her report in her last paragraph to Pound about Eliot cabling and giving the lawyer in New York full power of attorney for *The Waste Land*. What else have you got?"

Jane turned the pages to the letter dated July 19, 1922, from T.S. Eliot addressed to Ezra Pound. She handed the book back to Dr. Jansen and pointed to the relevant paragraph so he could take a look at it. "There's a letter Eliot wrote Pound three weeks later where he talks about the care he has to give to Vivien, his first wife. He minces her food to the point where it is liquefied practically, especially the meat. She has to take sealed medical milk, vitamins and proteins."

"Purified food is absorbed into the bloodstream more quickly than solid food. So is anything liquid or added to the food," Dr. Jansen stated and he glanced down at the text. He was silent for a minute before Jane continued.

"If you read a little farther, Eliot writes that they had her teeth examined but the doctors couldn't find anything wrong. In *The Waste Land*, there's a famous scene in a pub where two working class Englishwomen discuss the abortion of another woman they know. The woman had the abortion by just buying something at the chemist's, obviously poisonous. The woman's teeth were ruined afterward and her husband couldn't stand to look at her."

Dr. Jansen listened intently while Jane made her final point.

"T.S. Eliot is believed to have been gay. How does a gay man know so much about abortions in those days through chemical poisoning if he hasn't been looking into it himself? You can't tell me that that just dawned on him one day to include in *The Waste Land*. Abortions have always been the domain of women. It was our secret world. He had to have looked into this somehow to get information like that. And the coincidence about the teeth is just too uncanny, too hauntingly close."

"Deteriorating dental and mental health are symptoms of heavy metal poisoning. All of these symptoms are, including her diagnosis of colitis."

"Would you be willing, as a medical doctor, to make a statement for my PhD that these symptoms should be reexamined because they are symptoms of poisoning?"

"Sure, I can sum up the symptoms. Any doctor should recognize them immediately especially when symptoms like this seem to linger but don't seem to clear up or be caused by an acute illness. But if I was her family, I'd have her body exhumed and a new autopsy performed to test for toxins, especially heavy metal toxins, in her body."

“We can't make any sweeping accusations, but we can suggest a revaluation,” Jane added.

“Absolutely, I agree,” Dr. Jansen concurred.

Lisa and Danielle had disappeared with Jane's husband and her brother-in-law for four days. Jane sat behind the computer, surfing on the internet looking for clues, clues of anything. Darkness fell so early, and before she knew it, only the light of the Christmas tree lit up the room.

Her husband had been served the divorce papers ten days ago, which was quickly followed by a subpoena from the district attorney to discuss a possible community service sentence because the evidence was overwhelming to convict him of battery. He would also have to attend social rehabilitation classes. The subpoena stated that if he did not appear at the appointed time at the district attorney's office, the case would go to court and the sentence could be much harsher. When the police had called her husband in for questioning, he had confessed to punching her in the breast and slamming the door on her. His confession was necessary for further prosecution. Without it, even with the overwhelming forensic evidence, Jane's complaint would have been dismissed because of lack of evidence.

When Jane met with her attorney, her attorney didn't want to include the battery complaint or the district attorney's subpoena in the divorce proceedings. So Jane did as she had promised herself and found another attorney who would, and who Jane knew would stick by her and the children through thick and thin.

Jane's new attorney called a meeting between Jane and her husband to discuss the children and living arrangements during the divorce. After waiting half an hour, Jane and her attorney realized he wasn't going to show up.

Jane called him to ask him where he was.

"My brother is on his way up from Brussels."

"Your brother? Why?"

"He offered to help me out."

Jane hung up and told her attorney. "There's a family rumor that his brother used to beat up on their sister. She has been in and out of psychiatric care her whole life and refuses any contact with him. I don't know what is true, but I do know for sure his brother is explosive all the time, not just passive aggressive."

"Jane, go get the children and go stay with someone. There's no reason why his brother should be here."

Just then, Jane's phone rang. It was Dr. Jansen's office. Jane answered and heard Dr. Jansen ask, "Jane, are you ok?"

"Yeah, I'm at my new attorney's office to discuss the divorce. My husband didn't show up. Would you mind if I put it on speaker phone?"

"Not at all. Your attorney should hear this. I'm not supposed to discuss this with you because your husband is also a patient of mine, but something's up and I'm worried about your safety and the children's."

"We think something is going on, too. My husband didn't show up for the appointment to discuss the children and the living arrangements until the divorce is final, so we called him and he told us he was waiting for his brother to arrive from Brussels."

"What does his brother have to do with it? What's he doing here? Look, Jane, your in-laws just called me and tried to convince me that you needed psychiatric help and that I should have you committed because you were threatening suicide."

Jane and her attorney looked at each other, astounded.

Dr. Jansen continued, "But that's not all. When I told them that I didn't feel that was medically necessary and advised them not to get involved, they said they were going to drive here and take you back to their house to calm you down. In the meantime, they asked me to contact you and convince you to commit yourself because you trust my opinion. I flatly refused to do any such thing again because I felt there was no medical reason for it. I advised them that if they picked you up and it was against your will, it would be abduction and kidnapping. A half an hour later, I received an email from your husband's aunt, who claimed she was a certified psychologist, and that I should have you committed."

Jane's attorney interjected, "Dr. Jansen, right? This is Inge van Meren, Jane's family law attorney."

"Yes, I've heard you're better than the last one."

"Thank you. Keep all of this and don't let it get into anyone else's hands. This is evidence."

"Will do. We have the conversation documented and I have the email here."

"Jane, will you release this to me since it's part of your medical records?"

"Yes, of course."

"Dr. Jansen?" Inge asked. "I'll have Jane sign the release form for only this part of her medical records and fax it over to you right away. We can use this in the divorce proceedings that psychological abuse from the family was so pervasive, it even permeated into Jane's social circles including her health care providers in an attempt to isolate and brand her as mentally unstable. That's an abuser's trade secret."

"Agreed. I've seen this before. Once I decided not to get involved and the guy killed the whole family, including young children. I've promised myself never to let that happen again even if it means breaking protocols. That's fine. Fax the signed release form over and I'll send it electronically and fax the evidence right back immediately. Jane, in the meantime, you've got to get yourself and the children to a safe place before his brother gets here. You have my mobile number for emergencies?"

"Yes, I do."

"Dr. Jansen? Inge again. I think we should exchange mobile numbers, too."

"Good idea. Put yours on the release form. Jane go ahead and give Inge my mobile number. Be safe and keep in touch every day."

"Ok. Will do." Jane turned off the phone and looked at her attorney.

"Jane, you need to go."

"Yes."

"Be safe. I want you to check in with me every morning before noon and five in the afternoon. If I don't hear from you, I'm going to call the police."

"Ok."

"Go now. Get the girls. Call me."

Jane grabbed her things and picked up the girls at their after-school daycare which was next to their school. She walked with the girls to a local pizza place and got a few slices so that they would have something for dinner. While Jane and her daughters were walking to the car that was still parked close to the after-school daycare building, her husband and his brother emerged from the doors of the building.

"Where are you going with the children, you crazy woman?" her husband's brother screamed as they came toward Jane and the girls.

"What are you doing here?" Jane asked her brother-in-law. "We don't see you for years and suddenly you just appear out of nowhere all the way from Brussels?"

"Give me the keys to the car!" her husband demanded.

"No! It's my car!" Her husband grabbed the keys that she held in her hand. The weak key ring was untwisted in the struggle to hold onto the keys that ensued between the two of them. Her husband pushed the point of the key ring into her hand and pulled it forward, scratching open her hand. Jane felt the keys slip from her injured hand and immediately her heart sank because she had lost her means to escape with the children.

"Look at my hand. Look what you've done," Jane murmured as she stumbled, clutching her bleeding hand.

"Mama! Mama!" screamed Lisa and Danielle. Her husband had grabbed their hands and was trying to pull them away but they kept twisting their little hands to try and get away from him and run to their mother. While her husband busied himself with the children, his brother rushed up to Jane, pulled her by her scarf toward him, yanking her neck toward him and placing her in a headlock.

"Stay away from her, she's crazy!" he yelled at the children.

"Mama! Mama!" Her children's screams pierced Jane's heart. She twisted her legs and lower body to try and free herself while her brother-in-law tightened the headlock and tried to lift her. Jane's husband ushered the children away into the dark park adjacent to the school and daycare center.

"You're going to the police, not him, you bitch!" Her brother-in-law screamed in her right ear.

"What are you doing there?" a man emerged from the park, his dog barking on a leash. Jane's brother-in-law suddenly loosened the headlock and let Jane fall to the ground. He followed his brother into the park and disappeared. Jane could no longer hear her daughters' screams and as her body dropped to the ground, so did her spirits seemingly descend into hell. Jane felt the wet earth absorb into her clothing as she sat on the ground and an icy chill crawled up her spine. Her head was spinning as much as it throbbed. Her neck seemed immovable.

The man walking his dog rushed up to her, the little terrier anxiously jumping on his hind legs, yelping and licking Jane's face. "Are you all right? Did he try to rob you?"

"No, that's my brother-in-law. He has a violent personality. My husband has a police record for domestic violence and they've taken my daughters."

"Oh God," said the man. "Let me call the police."

The police arrived and the man walking his dog gave a statement. Jane would have to file a complaint in the morning, the officer said. "What about the children?"

"He's the father," the officer said. "He's allowed to take them wherever he wants."

"He has a domestic violence record!" Jane pleaded.

"So, probably against you, not the children!"

"Those children are not safe! I saw what his brother-in-law was doing to her!" The man with the dog pleaded in chorus with Jane.

The officer refused to hear it. "You were trying to run away with the children," answered the officer curtly.

"And with good reason!" the man with the dog answered with a tone of disrespect in his voice.

Jane had to walk home, or rather limp home, in the dark through the park that evening. Her knee had been twisted in the struggle. The man with his dog did not own a car and the police refused to give her a lift, citing other responsibilities. There was a police dog in the backseat which neither the witness nor Jane could make out in the dark. It was a lame excuse, the man told her after the police left. He gave her his number since both of them would have to go to the police and so that she could claim he was a witness.

When Jane got home, the house was empty. They had disappeared completely. He hadn't taken anything with him, no children's clothes or food, so they weren't prepared. But he had a large extensive family throughout the country and in Belgium, so he had plenty of places to hide.

The next morning Jane filed her complaint against her husband and her brother-in-law. The police still refused to look for her daughters and Jane fretted all day about what she should do. At 6:00 in the evening, she called the State Department's emergency number in Washington D.C. to report the abduction of two American citizens, Lisa, aged five, and Danielle, aged three, by their father and uncle. Within an hour, the embassy called her and she related the whole case. The following day at 8:30 am sharp, the vice consul from the US Consulate in Amsterdam called her and offered all his help and contact information. They discussed the Dutch authorities' response. Immediately after she hung up with that vice consul, the US vice consul in Brussels called her and gave her the same contact information and asked for possible addresses of where the children could be in Belgium. It was obviously a coordinated effort between the two consulates. Jane gave him her brother-in-law's address and the vice consul said he would be sending the Belgian authorities there to see whether the girls were being held there.

The vice consul from Amsterdam checked in with Jane every day. Then, on Christmas Eve, the Dutch police called her.

"You stop talking to the Americans, you hear me?"

"You can be assured because of this phone call I know I am doing the right thing. I am a citizen of the United States and I have the right to speak to my consulate."

"You carry a Dutch passport, too."

"Still, I am a citizen of the United States and so are my daughters. We have the right to consular assistance. Good day, officer."

The phone clicked on the other end. Jane related the conversation to the vice consul and he assured her she was completely within her rights. "The US recognizes you as citizens of the United States everywhere, all the time, regardless of any other passport you or your children may carry. I cannot believe they do not consider this an abduction. Call me if you have any news any time, even during Christmas. I'll call you as soon as I hear anything. I know this sounds stupid, but Merry Christmas."

"Merry Christmas to you, too."

"Chin up, Jane. We'll get you through this. Play it smart if the police or anyone suspect contacts you. Call me right away."

"Ok. I will."

"Goodbye."

"Bye."

That was the last contact Jane had had with the outside world as she turned from the computer and stared at the Christmas tree lights and her daughters' unopened presents under the tree.

The day after Christmas, Jane decided to take matters into her own hands as much as she could. At 7:30 in the morning, she removed the caller identification from her phone and called her husband. It worked. He answered, apparently expecting a call from his brother or parents.

Jane heard his voice answer the phone, grumbly and muffled by sleep, "Hello?"

"Where are you keeping Lisa and Danielle? Let me speak to them immediately!" Jane could hear Lisa's voice in the background shout excitedly to her little sister Danielle, "Danielle, Mama's on the phone with papa!" Jane heard Danielle answer back equally excited, "Mama!"

Then Jane heard Lisa's angelic voice through the phone as he let his daughter speak into it. "Mama, we're staying at Aunt Karin's house in the attic!" The same aunt who had sent the email to Jane's doctor, Dr. Jansen, claiming she was a psychologist and urging him to have Jane committed for psychiatric treatment.

It's just like the vice consul said and the operator on the State Department's emergency line in Washington said, Jane thought. They're all in on it together.

As soon as Lisa revealed their location, Jane's husband screamed into the phone, "So are you happy now? Did you get what you want, you bitch!" The phone clicked and the connection was cut off.

Jane immediately called the vice consul and then the police to give them the location of the children and to tell them that her husband was now answering his phone. "I'll call you as soon as I have some news, Jane," the vice consul promised. By the end of the day, the vice consul informed Jane that her husband would be bringing the girls home that evening and that if he did not, to contact him immediately and the State Department would continue to put its full weight behind her case. "He and his family who participated in this abduction have now been blacklisted for travel to the United States."

Jane, who had been afraid to ask the question, decided to ask it now. "Is there any possibility I could go back now? It's obvious he's a danger to both the children and me. I didn't want to mention this before, but when the children get home from school and I hear them playing, I've heard them discussing my funeral. They're three and five."

The vice consul was silent and the knowledge of this now weighed on him heavily. He knew it was just going to get worse until she and the children could get out. "I know Jane, that's dangerous. But if you go back to the States without a Dutch court's permission or full custody, you'll be in violation of The Hague Convention on International Child Abduction and the children will be sent back to him regardless of the underlying circumstances."

"But you know, the Dutch courts won't give me permission to leave or give me full custody either. My attorney told me, and she's willing to tell you, Frankenstein's monster always retains custody here, regardless of previous behavior or even criminal convictions."

"Jane, if you flee, the situation will be far worse. I've seen it happen. You've got to stay as it stands now until the girls are sixteen."

"I know."

"But keep playing it smart, Jane. You've got our support. Stay in touch with us regularly. Let us know everything. And one more thing."

"Yes?"

"Be careful of the police here. We know they don't enforce their domestic violence laws or finance their shelters adequately. They think they're good at window dressing. You're not the only American woman we have to look out for. Play it smart with everybody, the police, the courts, social services. You've got a good attorney now. Stick with her."

"Ok."

"Now you've got to go. The girls will be home soon."

As Jane hung up with the vice consul, her spirits sunk because of how daunting the future looked. The vice consul had tried to give her a pep talk, a common tactic whenever someone was trying to distract you from how bad the situation really was.

"Play it smart, Jane," echoed through her mind. And so Jane realized that the greatest nation on earth did not have her back, or her children's. And so she realized that the greatest nation on earth did not have the backs of its most vulnerable citizens in domestic violence situations overseas which undeniably and uncompromisingly resembled combat.

And so Jane came to realize that the greatest nation on earth still considered the inalienable right of safety for women and children to cease where the traditional domain of patriarchal privilege began, and the constitutional rights so championed by her nation were not meant for her and her daughters, especially when another nation did not respect them either.

Shame, Jane thought. All men are created equal is good diplomacy, but not all women and children. Shame, abomination.

Just then the phone rang. It was the Dutch police. "We found the children!" the officer on the other end announced. As Jane listened to the keystone cop with disgust, her husband pulled up with the children in the car. "I've got to go," she said apologetically. "My daughters are at the door," and hung up the phone. Lisa had unbuckled herself immediately and was already opening the car door. Danielle was trying to push the button to open her car seat but was not strong enough to get it open. Both of them yelled and shouted, "Mama! Mama!" and Jane opened the same door to let them in that her husband had slammed into her breast.

Two weeks later, her husband's right to live in the house was revoked by a Dutch judge until the divorce was final. Her husband moved into a house half a block away. There was nothing Jane could do about that. According to Dutch law, he could live wherever he wanted.

Jane was meeting with her advisor. Something had come up and he asked to meet with her personally. Jane feared he might be ill again, but that was not it at all.

"Jane, I met with Leif Leifson the other day. You know that book on Modernism he coordinated and wanted to publish you in?"

"Yeah."

"Well, it's about to be published any day now. I'm on the final editorial board and just last week I saw your name and chapter in the table of contents. Leif told me yesterday your chapter was pulled against his wishes. He did everything in his power but John Lebenstein couldn't be convinced you had an argument. He's on the peer review committee which steers the funding of the whole project."

"What? But he's my first reader." Jane could not hide how stunned she was. She wondered when the next carpet would be pulled out from under her feet.

"I know. This explains why you didn't get the funding in Leiden. I sent him to the meetings in my place. I thought I could trust him. Obviously, neither of us could. Jane, I'm going to send him a letter on Louvain letterhead today demanding he help you finish your PhD. As a newly appointed professor, he has no excuse not to help you since he has no other PhD candidates."

"I can't believe it," Jane's sense of betrayal was multiplied by the confession she had made to Dr. Lebenstein three months earlier. She felt her embarrassment and shame burn in her cheeks and in the pit of her stomach.

"Jane, I'm betting he's going to refuse to help you. And that's fine, but I don't want to suddenly exclude him because he'll know somebody tipped us off. I want him to step down himself. I don't want him knowing what you discovered on Eliot and Pound, nor anything else that might come up." Jane and Professor Stanford looked at each other, knowing which other American Modernist poet he was referring to, though he didn't say it outright. "If we couldn't trust him in the early stages of your work, there's no way we can trust him now."

Jane gave Professor Stanford a worried stare. "I think you may be right about that."

"Oh, I know I'm right. I'm going to write the letter to let him know you aren't alone in this. But expect a refusal. I am, anyway, and that's ok, then we can move on. In the meantime, I'm going to start looking for another first reader for you. At least, we know now and we can move on," he repeated.

"I'm really sorry about your publication. Now we know why he was so keen to translate your article into Dutch for the Dutch publication. Obviously, a publication in English would have gotten you much more exposure. I'm really sorry, Jane. Please don't let this slow you down or hold you back."

"I won't. I promise." Jane wondered how much more of the obvious she would naively disregard and how many battles would be fought over her head unbeknownst to her. As she listened to Professor Stanford, she felt ashamed that she had not had the eyes to see the truth about so many things in her life, but instead only seemed to have eyes for the unspeakable truths of others who rested on the pedestal of grandiose reputations that so far managed to protect them indefinitely.

O foolish girl
Playing chess with the gods again
On your own

Oh woe to you
Bold girl
Too brazen for your station

Woe to you
Be wary of the wrath to come when you
Like the physician and the poet
Play chess with the One and Only True God.

Oh hear the cries of maternal lamentation
Oh hear the cries of woe

As Professor Stanford predicted, Dr. Lebenstein had refused Professor Stanford's request to continue to be the first reader of her PhD and to provide her with the scholarly help she needed to continue and be successful in the academic world. Though his refusal surprised neither of them, Jane always liked to ask people who turned her down to tell her why face-to-face because then she could discern whether their reasons were truthful or just political bullshit. If they repeated the same thing that was in their letter or email with conviction, then it might be something she could learn from, was her theory. But if there was a discrepancy between what was on paper and what they told her unprepared, she knew instantly that she had cornered them into a tight spot and they were trying desperately to find any way out they could. Jane decided to apply the same tactic to Dr. Lebenstein.

Jane took her daughters with her. She decided to show them how to grill a professor. Personal titles, she wanted to teach her daughters, were never something that should ever keep you from questioning. Personal titles were only daunting if you let them daunt you. Question authority, she wanted to teach them, only then can you verify the validity of that authority. If an authority has a reason for being an authority, it should have nothing to fear from mere questioning.

Jane and her daughters arrived at the English department and Jane saw on the attendance board that Dr. Lebenstein, or rather Professor Lebenstein, was in. He had apparently already had his title changed on the attendance board even though he had not held his inaugural address, yet. Jane and her daughters climbed the stairs to his office. When they arrived at his door, a young female student stood at his desk demurely, asking him a question, and Professor Lebenstein looked up and answered her slowly with a deep voice, almost fatherly, and the young student basked in his paternal approach.

Jane stood in the doorway with Lisa on one side and Danielle on the other and she raised her eyes to look askance but directly at Professor Lebenstein. He got the message immediately that his current appointment was over and his next appointment was about to begin. You chameleon, thought Jane. You can't change your color under my gaze.

"I'm sorry, we need to stop. My next appointment has arrived." Lisa and Danielle knew exactly what to do and obediently walked over to the couch in Professor Lebenstein's office and sat on the edge back straight and upright, ready to listen attentively. Jane took the chair which stood opposite Professor Lebenstein's desk. The demure student left. Professor Lebenstein bellowed, trying to regain control of the situation, "My goodness, a whole delegation!" He didn't need to be introduced to the children. He knew exactly who they were. He had sent Jane a card when they were born.

AND THE LOG STARTS HERE.

"Good afternoon, Professor Lebenstein."

"Good afternoon, Miss Hooper."

"You know why I am here."

"Yes, I do."

"Well then, you know what my next question is."

He sat silently and she saw instantly that the liveliness in his blue eyes dissipated.

Jane waited an extra few seconds and then sprung the question on him, "Why?"

He waited and then answered, "It took me eighteen years to get where I wanted to be. There can be only one at a time. There can only be one Eliot and one Pound."

She knew where he was going. Jane decided to help him reach his destination so she could be sure. It was obvious Professor Stanford had mentioned her recent discovery to him, thinking he could be trusted. "Only one Eliot and one Pound? I see."

He, feeling pinned under her questioning stare, tried to redeem himself and cover up what he knew, "Yes, well, I read their biographies."

"Their biographies?" Jane questioned curtly.

"Yes, you know, the poets' biographies. Don't you read them?" he was struggling to regain control of the conversation. Jane's daughters watched attentively in silence.

"No. I don't read biographies of poets. I get everything I need to know from the poetry."

Astounded, he repeated, "You don't read biographies?"

"I read biographies of heads of state. Not poets. I get everything I need to know from the poetry."

Sensing the challenge in her words and her dark stare, Professor Lebenstein retreated and sank back in his chair a bit.

"Perhaps you can elaborate." He rested his elbow on the armrest of his chair and rested his chin on his middle finger while he rose his pointer to rest along his cheek up to his temple.

"In the final chapter of my dissertation," Jane said, "I discuss how Pound was able to shape Eliot's poetry through his editing. The poem in the manuscript of *The Waste Land* is so different from what was finally published, that it is essentially a separate poem entirely. Because of Pound's intervention, ultimately he even gave the poem its title that we know today, Pound recognized Davidson's and Thomson's overriding voices in Eliot's poetry and eliminated them especially in the first page of the manuscript, which is distinctly Davidsonian in voice and tone. The original title, 'He Do the Police in Different Voices', is distinctly Davidsonian and the entire first page Pound crossed out alludes overtly to Davidson's poetical technique in 'Thirty Bob a Week' and other Davidson poems. Pound saw this and eliminated other poets' voices that clouded out Eliot's voice too much. Eliot still carries the appropriation of these predecessors in his own work, but it is how he applies his inheritance of their work in his own that gives him his own poetic style and voice. No one can escape the roots that clutch. Eliot uses the same poetic strategies as his predecessors, as Pound did in his own work. But Eliot needed Pound to eliminate the inheritance from his predecessors when the burden of that inheritance became too overriding and suffocated his own voice. *The Waste Land* would not have been *The Waste Land* without Pound's edits. We all know that now. But how we can know how Pound shaped Eliot's work lies in how much we know about Eliot's English-language predecessors, who were also Pound's predecessors. Pound, unlike us, would have immediately recognized when their voices became too controlling over Eliot's and when he had to eliminate them to release Eliot's true poetic voice."

While she spoke, Professor Lebenstein's crystal blue eyes welled up with tears of love. He was silent after she finished speaking, but finally, he asked, his voice cracking, he asked, "Is it final yet?" Lisa and Danielle observed everything intently in silence. Children do not miss a thing.

"What, my dissertation or my divorce?"

"Both."

"Both are nearly final."

"Who is your first reader?"

"That is up to Professor Stanford."

"Who took you to Louvain," Professor Lebenstein responded angrily and looked away. The sudden revelation of his jealously was a victory even Jane had not expected. "Well, neither of you can get around me.

I am the only Pound expert on this side of the Atlantic. Neither of you will be able to circumvent me."

"Why should I stay here?" Jane asked softly. "This place sort of reminds me of Salem. You know, the same place where Eliot's ancestors hung witches for their own gain. People who were completely innocent hunted down and hung as witches."

He looked at her, panicking, "Where will you go?"

"That's a good question. Wherever I want. The world is a big place."

"I thought you couldn't leave," he pleaded.

"Lisa and Danielle, time to go. Your soccer practice will be starting soon." The girls rose from the couch while their mother rose from her seat to leave Professor Lebenstein's office.

"Soccer practice?" Professor Lebenstein stuttered.

"Time to go, girls." Jane turned towards the door and opened it. A newly appointed tutor stood in front of her and looked at her surprised.

"Oh excuse me, I didn't know John had visitors."

"Neither did I," Jane answered. Lisa and Danielle followed her out the door while the new tutor stepped aside to let them pass.

"Are those lovely girls your daughters?" the new tutor asked Professor Lebenstein cheerfully.

Professor Lebenstein rose from his seat and walked to his office door and watched Jane and her daughters leave. "No, I only have one daughter," Jane heard him answer as she and her daughters walked towards the stairwell to descend back into the outside world.

Neither Jane nor her daughters looked back as they turned the corner to take their first steps downstairs.


    OOOOOHHHHH professor
    What have you to fear from three little witches
    When there were more Modernists to consider?

    Oooohhh classicist
    In your ivory tower so concentrated on Europe
    When you should have looked West and also
        considered Williams

    O woe to you, myopic man
    Your student you underestimated has outperformed you
    Innately.

Jane and her daughters were visiting her dad for the last day. The next day they would fly back to Jane's mom's house near Philadelphia. Stopping off in Philadelphia gave Lisa and Danielle a chance to see their grandmother as well as a needed break before the long trip back across the Atlantic.

Jane's visit had been good for her and her daughters. Her family pampered her and her daughters after her ordeal, though both they and she knew the ordeal was long from over. As is common in divorces where domestic violence has taken place, the abuser uses stalking, the court system and the custody over the children to control the victim after the separation. Now that the divorce was final, Jane's ex-husband was stalking her constantly and she knew she would be back in court soon to plead for her and her children's safety. Though the judge in her divorce recognized her ex-husband's abusive behavior, Jane still had to comply with the unsupervised visitation schedule so that the judge did not suspect her of being manipulative and keeping the children from their father, even though she knew it was not safe for them. If Jane said what she really felt to a new judge, or any judge for that matter, she might not get the sympathy she got this time and she and her attorney knew that. Jane was caught between how she could best protect her children or how, if she did, matters might get much worse. Jane didn't know who or what she should fear more: her ex-husband and his family, or the judicial system.

Jane knew he and his family would use the children in some way to punish her for standing up for herself and the children. Jane feared so for her daughters when they were gone, she hadn't even noticed that she had stopped eating while they were gone. Her stomach shrank and she naturally ate less when they were there, too. She had lost fifty pounds in less than six months. Her clothes fell off of her emaciated body.

Jane had tried to exercise to feel better, but Dr. Jansen told her she needed to gain some weight back first. When she tried to eat more, it brought her so close to vomiting because her stomach had shrunk so much, she would eat even less at the next meal, if she ate at all. Since her children were gone almost every weekend, she had lost her passion for good food and cooking, as there was no one to cook for on the weekend. The girls loved good healthy food, too, but because of their size, they didn't eat much. When they ate together, Jane made smaller portions for herself, too, not only because she couldn't finish the food otherwise, but money was so tight that she couldn't bring herself to throw one morsel of food away.

Being with her family, both her mom and dad gave Jane, Lisa and Danielle a well-deserved break from the abuse and the stress. As soon as she landed in the States, the stress left her body and an enormous weight seemed to be lifted off of her. Jane was very grateful her family had collected the money together to give her and the girls this trip. So shocked were her family members when they saw how emaciated she had become because of the stress, that Jane's mom and her stepmother made her her favorite foods she couldn't get overseas. Though Jane was the black sheep in the family most of her life, by giving her this trip, her family let her know she and her daughters were still part of the flock no matter what. Knowing this was one of the few comforts Jane could relish lately, she made the most of it.

While she was in Georgetown, close to Austin, Texas, she asked her dad whether she could drive in with him to work in Austin and visit the manuscript library at the University of Texas.

"Sure! Going to get some work done?"

"Well, I'm here. I might as well see if there's anything here. Oh, by the way, would you mind taking a look at my first draft?"

"Sure! Be glad to!"

Just as her visit to the Beinecke at Yale had done, Jane found more than she had ever expected. In fact, she discovered that one of Pound's letters had been lost. Jane had requested to see the letter Pound had sent around the world to solicit funding for Eliot so that he could leave his day job at a bank, commonly known as the "Bel Esprit" letter. Pound vouched for Eliot as a poet and writer and clearly had stuck his neck out for Eliot. The manuscript library in Austin contained the only original. Jane opened the folder which should have contained the letter. It did not contain the letter, it contained a notice in red print that read, "MISSING: NOT RETURNED AFTER MODERNIST EXPOSITION".

"Why was it gone?" Jane thought. She remembered reading Eliot had been embarrassed by Pound's efforts to help him, but hadn't Eliot been complaining to Pound about how difficult his life was because he had to care for his sick wife as well as work at the bank? Jane realized now it was a smokescreen to gain and control Pound's confidence and trust while Eliot sent the manuscripts to John Quinn and secured his copyright of *The Waste Land*. This letter showed that Pound was willing to put his reputation on the line, which at that time was greater and more influential than Eliot's, to give Eliot the chance he needed to develop as a poet. If Eliot wanted to distance himself from Pound, letters of support from Pound before Eliot had his big break would not be convenient.

Jane began to get that uncanny feeling that this was a complete betrayal. Her next discovery confirmed that. Sensing that the missing manuscript had been overlooked by the head librarian, she decided not to report it immediately. She decided to request some of Eliot's letters that were there. One of them was addressed to Dorothy Shakespear, one of Pound's wives, and was dated 1946. This date meant that is was not yet published. Jane had to see this one.

Dorothy Shakespear had written Eliot and asked for his help to get Pound removed from St. Elizabeth's in Washington D.C. It was clear that after being captured by American forces in Italy after doing radio broadcasts for Mussolini, Pound was going to be tried as a traitor and if found guilty, he most certainly would have been executed. The only other option was to be declared insane with the hope of being transferred to another mental institution where he would not be essentially waiting to be tried.

Eliot gave Dorothy Shakespear the political run around. What could he do from London? Weren't people at Cornell trying to help Pound? Eliot, he assured Dorothy Shakespear, was helpless in this situation and the circumstances were beyond his control.

Then, the viciousness of his politics became clear to Jane when she noticed one of Eliot's handwritten messages at the bottom of the letter:

"Thank Ezra for the cutting."

Jane knew this not only referred to the process of editing as cutting, but also to the poem "Sage Homme". Pound had written the poem in his letter dated December 24, 1921, to Eliot to commemorate their collaboration on *The Waste Land*, which Eliot had promised to include when *The Waste Land* was published, just like he had promised Pound that his contribution to the poem would be recognized. Eliot had lied on all accounts. Jane looked up the poem again in the edition of Eliot's published letters that was at the library. There she read again in the first three stanzas of "Sage Homme":

These are the Poems of Eliot
By the Uranian Muse begot;
A Man their Mother was,
A Muse their Sire.

How did the printed Infancies result
From Nuptuals thus doubly difficult?

If you must needs enquire
Know diligent Reader
That on each Occasion
Ezra performed the caesarean Operation.

The "cutting" not only referred to editing in general, but in this case, Eliot's remark also referred to Pound's own words when Pound referred to editing *The Waste Land* as performing a caesarean section. Here, even though Pound was in the depths of his despair, Eliot still managed to kick Pound down when Pound's life had reached the abyss. The man Eliot had met at the right place at the right time, who was essential to Eliot's career. Here, in this letter, Eliot would admit to Pound's contribution to *The Waste Land*, but not in public ever. Not until after three years after his death when the manuscripts, which by chance had been found in New York, were released to the public, did it become clear what Pound's contribution had been to what was considered the greatest poem of the twentieth century.

"Jesus, who's the real traitor?" Jane asked herself out loud which drew irritated glances from the librarian's desk. Eliot also became a Brit and took on an English accent, she thought, which now made scholars question whether Eliot was an American poet at all.

Without a doubt, Eliot was the traitor, Jane concluded to herself. She stood up and walked to the librarian's desk to request copies of everything. After she paid, Jane walked to the lockers, retrieved her bag and walked down the stairs to leave the building. She called her dad and asked him to pick her up.

"Sure I will. Did you get some work done?"

"Plenty."

"Good. We're going to dinner tonight with your uncle since it's your last night here with the girls. We have something to give you."

"Sounds good."

Jane, her daughters, her dad and his wife, and her uncle and her aunt sat around the table at the family-owned Mexican restaurant in downtown Georgetown. Everything had a real hometown feel about it. Everyone enjoyed the meal, but everyone's spirits were still dampened because Jane and her daughters were leaving the next day and Jane's dad had been diagnosed with cancer for the fourth time.

"It's just skin cancer again," her dad assured her after he had picked her up at the University of Texas, but Jane couldn't be reassured and started to cry. She could not deny the pervasive feeling that time was not on her side especially since, as it stood at that moment, she would not be able to go home until Danielle was sixteen, and that was twelve years away. She didn't know when she would see her family or her country again.

The waitress had just cleared the table when her uncle, her dad's younger brother, announced, "Jane, your dad and I wanted to give this to you when you defend your PhD, but we think you should have it now." He held up a book wrapped in plastic wrap. "We think you're the only person in the family who knows what to do with it." Jane sat at the opposite end of the long table from her uncle and he handed the book to his older brother, Jane's dad, who then passed it on to Jane.

Her uncle had mentioned to her once that he had a signed copy of the first edition of William Carlos Williams' autobiography. Jane unwound the plastic wrap from around the book. Funny to use kitchen utensils to protect something that one of the greatest poets of the twentieth century had signed, Jane thought. Just like her uncle. She opened the book.

Then she saw the book wasn't her uncle's. It was her grandmother's who had passed away ten years ago. Her stomach sank and her heart began to race.

Oh, good God.

The inscription inside revealed instantly that Williams and her grandmother were more than just doctor and patient. It read:

"Doris Hooper
For old times' sake.
William Carlos Williams
4/1/1952"

Jane looked up for a split second to see her father's face before she looked away to try and let this revelation digest. Her father was looking straight forward with a solid, blank stare. Jane looked away and tried to regain her composure before she thanked her uncle.

"Thank you all. That's very kind of you."

Lisa and Danielle noticed afterwards that their mother was eerily silent. They didn't understand what had happened, but they knew their mother was never as quiet as this. Something had happened, but they couldn't put their little fingers on just what it was.

Jane knew what happened. A tom cat had gotten her tongue. For the time being, she had lost her salt.

Beware!
Beware!
Beware of what you have wished for

O you who turn the wheel and look windward
Even though Yahveh, God, Allah has already written
    your destiny
In the wrinkles and creases of your forehead

Now you have drawn the Hanged Man.
The Lord, God Almighty has grabbed you by the collar
And yanked you up to see His Face
Screaming, "You are MINE!" which echoes now against
    the mountains

And there you hang
suspending
pending
awaiting His next move.

Foolish girl, oh
Foolish, westerner, stop your whining
We can't stand the sound and you cannot fight it
Your life was never your own
From even before its beginning

Earth's axle creeks
Not because it wants to but because it must.

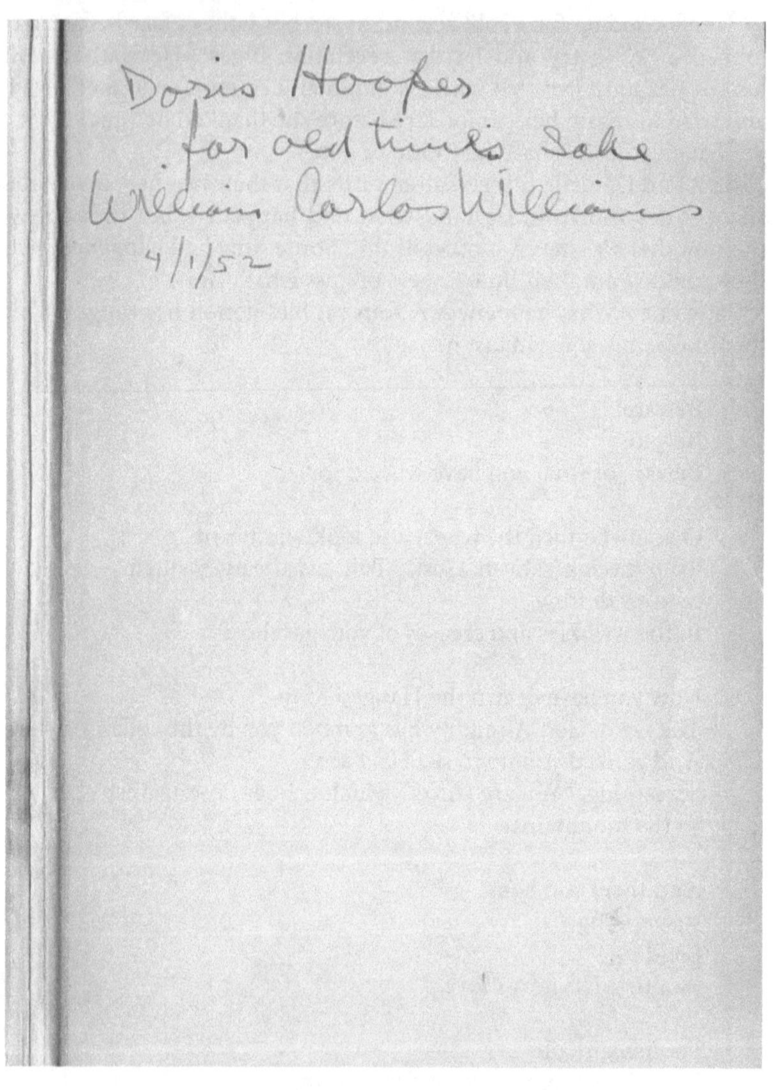


*William Carlos Williams' inscription to Doris Hooper
in the first edition of his autobiography.*

Jane sat next to her lawyer, Inge van Meren, in the courtroom while Inge summed up the reasons why Jane needed a restraining order against her ex-husband. In the Netherlands, both lawyers and judges wore the Geneva gown in the courtroom which made Jane think of Salem again. Her ex-husband's attorney had opened the hearing by trying to exculpate his behavior because, she said, Jane was paranoid and needed to be committed to an asylum.

The judge was not amused. She stopped the attorney and told her she had heard enough. Now the judge was listening to Inge's argument. Jane thought for a moment that maybe, just maybe, she had a chance, but she was so petrified that something might happen that she didn't expect, she kept staring at her hands in her lap.

Inge, who stood next to Jane while she addressed the judge, periodically looked down at Jane worriedly. She had never seen her so downtrodden.

Suddenly, the judge asked Inge to stop and said, "Let me address the plaintiff. Why do you want a restraining order? You are going to let the father see the children, aren't you?"

At least, Jane and Inge had expected this trap, and had prepared for it. Inge had coached Jane not to express her fears about the children's safety when they were with their father. That could be held against her.

"Of course, your honor."

"Good. Now why do you want this restraining order?"

"He waits in front of my door. I can't leave the house."

"We can give him a restraining order for your street." The judge had clearly not prepared for this hearing.

"But your honor, he lives in my street. I don't want to be abused again."

"What!" the judge screamed. "The abuse happened almost a year ago! Get over it!"

Jane sunk back into her chair. "Your honor, without a restraining order, the police cannot arrest him when he loiters around her house," Inge pointed out.

"Don't get smart with me in my courtroom!"

At this point Jane tuned out her surroundings completely and wondered why she had even bothered. Inge expressed her dismay to the judge at such a travesty of justice and the lack of protection her country was providing her client.

Years later, Jane discovered that at the very same hour of the very same day while she pleaded for her and her children's safety, Professor John Lebenstein, also dressed in Geneva gown but then as a professor in Leiden, gave his inaugural address. He spoke of the concept of Salem in various works of literature and how much he admired Pound. He thanked Professor Stanford for taking such a gamble when he took him, a classicist, on as a PhD student. He promised to continue where Professor Stanford had left off now that he was taking over his chair. Professor Lebenstein also said that he learned the most from his students, and while he taught them, he actually believed that he learned more from them than he ever could teach them himself. Professor Lebenstein expressed his utmost desire that this cross-pollination between him and his students would never end.

But Jane was not listening. After that day in February, Jane and Professor Lebenstein never saw each other again.

Jane was preoccupied with other priorities, like the safety of her and her daughters. Besides she had moved on to another Modernist poet. She had no choice. She must; that poet was calling her home.

You cannot sever the roots that clutch.

No one can, ever.

Jane had kept everything to herself for more than a year. Despite her talkative nature, she became secretive and at times even sullen after her dad had given her her grandmother's book with Williams' message in it. But it was not the message alone that had dampened her usually sparkling personality. Jane had, of course, looked into Williams' poetry. If Jane still tried to convince herself she could wallow in disbelief about her grandmother and Williams, her discovery of a poem by Williams entitled "Nantucket", written in early 1934 shattered any illusions of disbelief she still clung to.

Nantucket was the island off the coast of Massachusetts on which her father's mother had be born and raised. Her family had lived on Nantucket since the seventeenth century. It was the only thing her grandmother ever told Jane about her past and it was something she was extremely proud of. But it was not only her origins she was proud of; Jane knew her grandmother told her about Nantucket because it was that special trait that made her an identifiable figure in Williams' poetry in contrast to the other women. Jane's grandmother had also been a passionate English literature teacher at a Rutherford high school. When Jane's grandmother and Williams had discussed literature, she must have mentioned to him she was from Nantucket, a location so key to the American literary psyche.

The poem "Nantucket" had been written in early 1934. Jane's father had been born in early January, 1935. The poem, Jane read, was not a well-known poem and was usually considered to be an Imagist poem, even though Williams wrote it twenty years after the Imagist movement. But there was another way to read the poem: overtly Freudian. The sexual overtones abound undeniably in the poem, but it is also the beauty of the poem that strikes readers, even as it reminds them of the vile high school and college limerick, "There was a man from Nantucket, whose dick was so long he could suck it."

It was as if Williams was taking something stained and illegitimate for both him and Jane's grandmother, and rendering it into something beautiful and clean, a poem, as an act of redemption for both of them, especially her, so gripped by Puritanical roots.

Nantucket

Flowers through the window
lavender and yellow

changed by white curtains –
Smell of cleanliness –

Sunshine of late afternoon –
On the glass tray

a glass pitcher, the tumbler
turned down, by which

a key is lying – And the
immaculate white bed

Jane picked up the phone to call her advisor. She hadn't spoken to him
in over a year since he went to Harvard and she went to St. Louis to
present a paper on Eliot and Pound. Even though she had already
received the book from her father the last time she had spoken to
Professor Stanford, she didn't have the courage to tell anyone or talk
to anyone about it, even her trusted advisor. Instead, Jane had kept it
to herself for over a year, like an unwanted pregnancy one decides to
keep and accept. Something one must learn to embrace through time
because life will never be the same.

But now the time had come to tell the story because if poetry does
anything, it does not lie. Poetry and poets tell the unspeakable truths
no one wants to know. Now Jane knew, too, why Williams called *The
Waste Land* the worst catastrophe to English letters. Because he knew
its publication was based on a betrayal.

APPLICATION FOR MEMBERSHIP TO THE NATIONAL SOCIETY

OF THE

# DAUGHTERS OF THE AMERICAN REVOLUTION
WASHINGTON, D. C.

State *New Jersey*

City *Rutherford*

Name of Chapter *John Rutherford*

National Number *350463*

(Miss or Mrs.) *Mabel Turner Hussey*

Wife or Widow of *Elliot Benham Hussey*

Residence *134* *Summit Cross* *Rutherford* *New Jersey*
Number — Street — City — State

DESCENDANT OF

*Tristram Pinkham*

The undersigned have investigated and approved the applicant and her application.

*January 18th*, 194*5*

*Frances S. Steldeemer*
Chapter Regent.

*Ethel D. Liebensberger*
Chapter Secretary.

*Frances S. Wright*
Chapter Registrar.

Application and duplicate received by National Society *JAN 24 1945*, 194

Fees received by National Society *Jan. 24*, 194*5*

Application examined and approved *FEB 1 1945*, 194

*Estella A. O'Byrne*
Registrar General.

Accepted by the National Board of Management *FEB 1 - 1945* 194

*Marjorie R. Manlove*
Recording Secretary General.

Endorsement for membership at large:

State Regent.

Nominated and recommended by the two undersigned members of the Society in good standing, to whom the applicant is personally known.

### ENDORSED IN HANDWRITING BY

Name *Evelyn R. Holman*      Name *Grace Frances Brown*

Residence *42 Lincoln Ave*   Residence *96 Ridge Road*

*Rutherford, N.J.*            *Rutherford, N.J.*

When filled out and properly endorsed the application must be forwarded to the Treasurer General, N.S. D.A.R., Memorial Continental Hall, Washington, D. C., with the necessary fee and dues. When approved by the National Board, one copy will be returned to the Registrar of the Chapter or to the individual, if joining At Large, and the other will be filed with the National Society.

*Mabel Hussey's Daughters of the American Revolution application, 1945. Mabel Hussey is Doris Hooper's mother. This application traces Doris Hooper's roots on Nantucket back to 1665.*

I, *Mabel Turner Hussey* ............being of the age of eighteen
years and upwards, hereby apply for membership in the Society by right of lineal
descent in the following line from *Tristram Pinkham* ....................
who was born in *Nantucket, Mass* ....on the *24th* day of *June*, *1748*
and died in ............ *"* ............on the *13th* day of *June*, *1827*
His place of residence during the Revolution was *Nantucket, Mass* ....
(Please give all dates by numerals, month first, and given names in full)

1. I am the daughter of
*Abner Turner, Jr.* ....born on *3-18-1849* at *Nantucket, Mass*
died at *Nantucket* ....on *6-30-1896* and his (first or ) wife
*Susie Eliza Ray* ....born on *6-1-1853* at *Nantucket, Mass*
died at *Rutherford, N.J.* ....on *9-4-1921* married on *11-26-1873*

2. The said *Abner Turner, Jr.* ....was the child of
*Abner Turner* ....born on *8-24-1810* at *Nantucket*
died at *Nantucket* ....on *2-3-1881* and his (first or ) wife
*Lucina Randall* ....born on *12-16-1815* at *Chatham, Mass*
died at *Nantucket* ....on *9-12-1896* married on *12-15-1839*

3. The said *Abner Turner* ....was the child of
*Susannah Pinkham* ....born on *8-18-1770* at *Nantucket*
died at *Nantucket* ....on *12-14-1843* and his (first husband wife)
*Baker Turner* ....born on .... at *Nantucket*
died at *Nantucket* ....on *7-19-1815* married on *8-26-1793*

4. The said *Susannah Pinkham* ....was the child of
*Tristram Pinkham* ....born on *1-24-1748* at *Nantucket*
died at *Nantucket* ....on *6-13-1827* and his (first or ) wife
*Lydia Coffin* ....born on *7-17-1754* at *Nantucket*
died at *Nantucket* ....on *9-13-1818* married on *1-29-1767*

5. The said *Tristram Pinkham* ....was the child of
*Solomon Pinkham* ....born on *7-15-1710* at *Nantucket*
died at *Nantucket* ....on *9-26-1778* and his (first or ) wife
*Eunice Gardner* ....born on *1-29-1718* at *Nantucket*
died at *Nantucket* ....on *2-1-1787* married on *2-17-1736 or 6*

6. The said *Solomon Pinkham* ....was the child of
*Jonathan Pinkham* ....born on *9-12-1684* at *Nantucket*
died at *Nantucket* ....on *1736* and his (first or ) wife
*Hannah Brown Coffin* ....born on *4-6-1689* at *Nantucket*
died at *Nantucket* ....on *12-13-1730* married on ....

7. The said *Jonathan Pinkham* ....was the child of
*Richard Pinkham* ....born on .... at *Portsmouth, Isle of Wight*
died at .... on *1718* and his (first or ) wife
*Mary Coffin* ....born on *4-18-1665* at *Nantucket*
died at *Nantucket* ....on *2-1-1741* married on ....

8. The said ....was the child of
....born on .... at ....
died at .... on .... and his (first or ) wife
....born on .... at ....
died at .... on .... married on ....

9. The said ....was the child of
....born on .... at ....
died at .... on .... and his (first or ) wife
....born on .... at ....
died at .... on .... married on ....

*Mabel Hussey's Daughter of the
American Revolution application, p. 2, 1945.*

# REFERENCES FOR LINEAGE

(Proofs for line of descent are wills, administrations, deeds, church, Bible, census and pension records, tombstones, histories, genealogies, old newspapers, etc.)

Give below a reference to the authority for EACH statement of Birth, Marriage* or Death. If from published records, give names of books and page numbers. If from unpublished records, applicant must file duplicate certified or attested copies of same. *1st Gen — Nantucket V.R. Vol II p 597 (& Abner Jr)*

2nd Gen. *Nantucket Vital Records Vol III p 150-402-592 (& L & A)*

*Births* " Vol IV p. 375-312-353 477 (m & A)

3rd Gen. " " " *Vol II 402-597-382 (& B & S)*

*Marriages* " " " *Vol 4 p 287-477 (w 3 & S)*

4th Gen. *Deaths* " " *Vol 5 485-488 (& T & A)*

3rd *Vol I 246 (& L) Vol II 383 (& T) Vol III 246 (m T & A) Vol IV 576 (m T & A) 572-593*

5th Gen. *Vol I pp 592-593 (d. B. d. S.)*

6th Gen.

7th Gen.

8th Gen.

9th Gen.

Give, if possible, the following data: My Revolutionary ancestor was married
(1) to *Lydia Coffin* at *Nantucket* *1-29, 1767*
(2) to at , 1
(3) to at , 1

## CHILDREN OF REVOLUTIONARY ANCESTOR

(By each marriage, if married more than once)

| Names | Dates of Birth | To Whom Married, noting if Married more than once |
|---|---|---|
| *Esmira* | | |
| *Tristram* | | |
| *Jas* | | |
| *Susanna* | *8-18-1770* | *Baker Turner* |
| *Lydia* | *2-18-1781* | |
| | | |
| | | |
| | | |
| *Nantucket V.R. Vol II 373, 376, 382, 382* | | |
| " " *Vol IV 477* | | |

I was born on *3-4-1875* at *Providence, R.I.* married on *May - 1899* at *Nantucket* by *Rev. Geo. H. Badger* to *Elliot B. Hussey* who was born on *12-16-1874*

I do (or do not) give consent to the office of Registrar General to furnish by correspondence specific information to applicants seeking eligibility to membership on same or connecting lineage.

* Marriage in every instance in this paper means legal and lawful marriage.
Date of marriage may be substituted for dates of birth and death where such date proves the soldier to have been living during the Revolution and of a suitable age for service.
(Note: Resolution adopted by the Twenty-fourth Continental Congress:
Descendants of polygamous marriage are not acceptable as members of this Society.)

*Mabel Hussey's Daughter of the
American Revolution application, p. 3, 1945.*

## ELIGIBILITY CLAUSE.

"Any woman is eligible for membership in the National Society of the Daughters of the American Revolution who is not less than eighteen years of age, and who is descended from a man or woman who, with unfailing loyalty to the cause of American Independence, served as a sailor, or as a soldier or civil officer in one of the several Colonies or States, or in the United Colonies or States, or as a recognized patriot, or rendered material aid thereto; provided the applicant is personally acceptable to the Society." (Constitution, Article III, Section 1.)

### ANCESTOR'S SERVICES

My ancestor's services in assisting in the establishment of American Independence during the War of the Revolution were as follows:

*Tristram Pinkham's* [Patriot] *given in a list of the people of Nantucket, Mass. who helped the colonies in the Revolution by loaning funds. He could not go to war because of a disabled right hand. This list is published in the Third Report of the National Society, D.A.R. Oct. 1898 - Oct. 1900 pages 316 to 345*

*References for names & dates*
*Pollard Papers. Vol. 3 p. 190, 194 & 524*

The said *Tristram Pinkham* is the ancestor who assisted in establishing American Independence, while acting in the capacity of, *gave financial aid*

Give references by volume and page to the documentary or other authorities for—MILITARY RECORD: *Where reference is made to unpublished or inaccessible records of service, the applicant must file the official copy.*

Vol. *3* p. *337* *NSDAR Report - 1898-1900*

Vol. p.

The following form of acknowledgment is required:

Applicant further says that the said *Tristram Pinkham* (name of ancestor from whom eligibility is derived) is the ancestor mentioned in the foregoing application, and that the statements hereinbefore set forth are true to the best of her knowledge and belief.

The applicant also pledges allegiance to the United States of America and agrees to support its Constitution. This applies only to citizens of the United States of America.

(Signature of Applicant) *Mabel Turner Hussey*
(Kindly sign your name before the notary exactly as you wish it to appear on our records.)

Subscribed and sworn to before me at *Rutherford* , *New Jersey*
(City) (State)

this *15th* day of *January* A. D. *1945*

[SEAL]  ELIZABETH R. PLATT
NOTARY PUBLIC OF N. J.
My Commission expires Jan. 26, 1949

*Elizabeth R. Platt*
Signature of Notary.

*Mabel Hussey's Daughter of the
American Revolution application, p. 4, 1945.*

Jane and her dad took a trip to Rutherford to visit the town he grew up in and to see all the houses where he and his family had lived. Of course, they were also there to visit the Presbyterian church across from Williams' house where Jane was baptized; Williams' house and finally, the William Carlos Williams Center.

When Jane and her father entered the William Carlos Williams Center, her father was bombarded by the pictures of Williams that so much resembled his own face. In an instant, Jane's father disappeared. Jane did not know where he was until she heard the sobs coming from the men's room. Her father cried there for forty-five minutes.

Jane waited patiently in front of the confrontational pictures that portrayed Williams' celebratory life while her father mourned his own lesser-known, but in some ways, equally celebratory life as a journalist and lobbyist who was burdened by an unspeakable truth that the scarlet letter on his face could not hide. So he and everyone around him had to make up for that through the poetic strategies of silence and denial. Jane realized that that was how family secrets worked. Everyone, in unison, just acted like the secrets weren't there.

And Jane, in her solitude in front of the pictures of Williams, her father's sobs still audible in the distance, realized she could not escape her destiny just like her family's generations on both sides that had preceded her had not been able to either. Though they all tried time and time again to remain on the outskirts of history, they were sucked time and time again into the spinning vortex of its center.

No one can escape the roots that clutch.

Their tentacles are inescapable.

Jane took a picture of the sun's rays shining down on the Williams Center, which was the Faculty of Arts building at the University of Pennsylvania. Jane was nervous about her meeting with the first professor outside of her normal academic circle who she would tell her discoveries to. She had brought her grandmother's book with her which she carefully guarded in her purse under her right arm, just in case he didn't believe her.

Jane had prepared her scholarly argument that she believed this evidence showed why the Modernists, Eliot, Pound and Williams, clung so tenaciously to the concept of impersonal poetry just in case the professor got irritated with disbelief. Their personal lives were the inspiration for their work as is always the case in all art, she repeated in her mind. However, the Modernists had learned from the fates of their immediate literary predecessors, the late-nineteenth century British poets, that revealing the scandals of their lives through their art could also ruin their reputations with the British publishing establishment, which in turn had reacted against the British poets by not publishing them. The Modernists knew that if they were to survive in the public mind, they must not turn the publishers against them. Yeats had defended the British poets and Williams mentioned this in his autobiography. Eliot did his best to distinguish himself from the other American Modernist poets, and pandered to the British publishing establishment by becoming more English than an Englishman.

Ok. I'm ready, she said to herself.

During lunch, Jane never had to get to her scholarly argument. Her story was enough to grab the professor's attention and keep him listening.

# ACKNOWLEDGEMENTS

I would like to thank Kjeld de Ruyter for his undying loyalty and mesmerizing graphic design.

And to Musa Uslu who taught me to let nothing stop me from embracing my kismet.

May peace be upon you, Musa, always.